Once more, Bolan had proved his willingness to take a bullet for an ally

The Land Rover lurched, and with the odd plunk of a bullet striking the hardened skin of the big off-road vehicle, they were charging away from the battle scene.

The enemy had set up an ambush. It had taken alertness, luck, shooting skill and bald audacity to escape the attack.

But not before putting a few dozen into his enemies first.

The Land Rover charged over the broken road, escaping to let its occupants fight another day.

But Bolan knew the worrisome truth.

MACK BOLAN ®
The Executioner

The Executioner®
Don Pendleton's

SUICIDE
HIGHWAY

A GOLD EAGLE BOOK FROM
WORLDWIDE®

TORONTO • NEW YORK • LONDON
AMSTERDAM • PARIS • SYDNEY • HAMBURG
STOCKHOLM • ATHENS • TOKYO • MILAN
MADRID • WARSAW • BUDAPEST • AUCKLAND

First edition August 2005
ISBN 0-373-64321-7

Special thanks and acknowledgment to
Doug Wojtowicz for his contribution to this work.

SUICIDE HIGHWAY

Hatred and vengeance, my eternal portion,
Scarce can endure delay of execution,
Wait, with impatient readiness, to seize my
Soul in a moment.

—William Cowper 1731–1800
The Task

Hatred and vengeance are my eternal companions,
not because I choose to give in to them, but because
I oppose them. When my body falls and my soul is
seized, hatred and vengeance will have one less wolf
at their heels.

—Mack Bolan

To our soldiers still standing guard and
giving their all around the world.
Come home safe to your families.

1

Sofia DeLarroque shook her head. The wounds from an AK-47 couldn't have been more obvious if the shooter had circled each ragged hole in black marker and wrote "AK hit" with an arrow pointing to it.

The entry wounds were big enough to stick a finger into, and the bullets had cut completely through the body, their sharp steel cores plowing through muscle and bone like a boat hull through water, no deflection. Thankfully, there was little fragmentation or shrapnel. Truly dangerous bullets hit flesh and tore themselves apart, spinning missiles off the main track of the wound path. As it was, the child she was working on was bleeding badly, and she was running short on gauze to apply pressure bandages.

Welcome to day 216, she reminded herself.

Two hundred sixteen days in Afghanistan.

The American government claimed to have decisively beaten the supporters of the Taliban. So why did Americans and Afghans and international relief workers still come under attack on a daily basis?

Sofia wiped her brow, aware of the smear of gore she left on her platinum blond hair and her smooth, porcelain-like forehead. She could have been a model if she'd chosen to stay in France. She was tall, leggy, with just enough fullness of figure to give her deadly curves in all the right places. Crystal blue eyes that people said were perfect for seducing the camera instead were busy trying to evaluate how to best keep a psychopath's victim stable long enough to make it to a surgical table.

Same stuff. Different country.

Ethiopia.

Palestine.

Afghanistan.

All the lands she'd chosen held the same things in common. Thugs and violence causing pain and suffering to the weak and helpless.

The thought flashed across her mind like lightning, and she tried to put aside the mental image of other children, the same age as this one, screaming and twisting terribly as bullets ripped into them.

Shame crushed Sofia as she gripped the girl's hand, looking into her big, watery brown eyes. Tears glistened on the girl's olive cheeks as thin, weak lips moved noiselessly.

"It's all right," Sofia whispered. She stroked a few strands of thick, black hair from the girl's forehead, fighting off the memories that had been dogging her heels for exactly two hundred thirty-eight days and nine hours.

Images of grim murderers dressed head-to-toe in black, sweeping automatic weapons across fleeing, unarmed refugees in a Palestinian camp. The sound of cloth tearing echoed the distant sounds of bullet-spitting slaying machines as bodies were swept off their feet and flung cruelly, mercilessly into bloody rags.

Her body tensed against the sound of the shredding fabric, trying to fight off the memories of the murders she'd witnessed. Murders she'd witnessed while huddled under the wreckage of a tent, flames licking all around her, as she muffled the face of a child against her bosom. Around them, shadows charged and darted, backlit by flames.

There was no mistaking it.

The men were on a mission of retribution. Only days before, a restaurant had been blown to hell by a suicide bomber. One madman's act taking almost two-dozen lives and injuring tens more. A temporary cease-fire ended with rock throwing and riots and an assault on the refugee camp at Shafeeq.

When asked later she claimed not to have seen any faces.

She hadn't been convincing enough because a salvo of gunshots only barely missed her. The UN pulled her and the other workers out as quickly as they could, finding a new territory for them to work.

It was unlikely anti-Palestinian forces would find refuge and assistance in Afghanistan.

Sofia held the girl's hand as the doctor checked on her anesthesia's progress.

It was unlikely that the hard-faced men she saw in the shadowy camp would follow her halfway across a continent, but she still sweated with terror each day, more intensely in recent times.

"THIS IS THE FIRST ONE we've even gotten anything on," Greb Steiner said softly as he threaded the sound suppressor onto the muzzle of his Beretta. Olsen Rhodin often wondered at the mannerisms of the hard-core soldier, a man whose face and hands betrayed the violence of his life in a road map of scar tissue. He never raised his voice and rarely expressed anger or hostility. At times, Rhodin wondered if Steiner lived in a constant state of sadness, his brow bent with guilt.

Then again, Rhodin had watched Steiner shoot weeping mothers point-blank in the face just to send a message to their husbands.

Maybe it was guilt that weighed on Steiner's face and voice. But it never stopped him from doing the job of protecting their country.

"We'll find the others. Don't worry," Rhodin said. "We have the whole team here. They'll find the others."

Steiner chambered a .22-caliber slug into the Beretta, then holstered the piece. He was to be the executioner, again.

It was a role that Steiner was suited for. This was a man who would die before he talked, if ever he could be captured alive. A brick of a man, square, hard and rough, he towered a couple of inches over six feet, and his dark eyes seemed reddish, as if swimming in the blood he'd spilled over the course of his career. He slipped out of the truck with an agility that belied his blocky form.

Rhodin dropped down. He didn't dramatically check the chamber of his rifle like the men with them did. He was a professional, and had locked and loaded the weapon as soon as he'd received it back at their improvised headquarters. Rifle shells pinged from breeches as "veteran" Taliban soldiers made themselves feel good with a spit of macho masterbatory gun manipulation.

"A waste of ammo," he said under his breath, in English so the Afghans wouldn't understand.

Steiner heard him and shrugged. "What? The rounds on the ground, or them?"

Rhodin shook his head. "Both."

Steiner sighed, as if a greater load was added to the world-sized weight on his shoulders. "Let's go."

SOFIA'S HEART SANK as Dr. Gibson hung his head. Green streaks smeared across the monitor's brownish black surface, the telltale whine of a flatline speaking the grim reality of another life lost. It wasn't new, this horrifying change from a vibrant, living child full of the desire to play, learn and love to a cooling lump of motionless meat on a cold, metal surgical table.

"Let's get the next one in here," Gibson muttered, the harshness in his voice sounding like a body dragged across gravel. He was tearing off his blood-splattered gloves and pulling on fresh, sterile latex to keep infections from passing along.

Sofia looked down at the innocent face, gone from a healthy olive tone to almost bone-white from blood loss. The dead girl resembled an angel.

Les innocentes, the name for children who died with no spot of sin on their souls, going immediately to heaven, whatever heaven they believed in, if they knew that much at their age. Sofia wondered if heaven really existed, then dismissed the thought as she wheeled the body away to make room for a fresh victim.

Certainly a heaven had to exist.

Because this was hell.

She stopped as she reached the improvised morgue, leaving the table parked against a half-dozen others, lined up tightly to make the most of the space available until they could arrange burials. Their job was to make sure that the living survived. Respect for the dead would have to wait a few minutes, a few hours, until those who needed help got it.

The cart rolled as she let go of it, metal clanking dully against other metal, the tabletops covered with the wrapped-up remains of those who couldn't be saved. Seven lost so far. That was just this day.

Sofia closed her eyes.

Seven added to the hundreds she had already seen.

Seven added to the mountain of dead she'd watched either die in the care of the medical mission, or gunned down directly by madmen on a crusade. Her jaw clenched as she tried to suppress her rage, her impotence at a world where juggernauts rolled over the helpless, smashing them to a pulp in the street, leaving dead and maimed in their wake.

She considered it a perversion of the concept of a trinity. Man fathered the gun. The gun sought to please its creator, so the gun gave man power. Man lusted after the power. Gun slew man's children.

The unholy trinity continued to rampage across the face of the earth like a cancer. All she could do was help pick up the pieces, try to keep the wounded from being the dead and to reassemble the maimed.

It was a Band-Aid trying to cover an amputation. The stump was gushing blood, and the United Nations was holding up one sandbag in the middle, watching in despair, maybe in disbelief as currents slushed around on either side. A wave of sickness hammered into Sofia as she whispered a torrent of "damns" under her breath, pounding her hand against the trolley's handlebars, until she realized that people in the hall were staring at her.

Her voice was hoarse, and her hand felt like someone had taken a maul to it. She'd be lucky if she hadn't broken bones. Her eyes burned, face raw from tears.

The two staff members outside the door looked at her, a combination of fear and sympathy fighting for control of their features, and Sofia wished she were dead right then, shame and guilt boiling up into her throat, a new wave of tears ready to rise.

"I'm sorry," she whispered.

One of her fellow aid workers, Charles, took a tentative step forward. "It'll be okay, Sofia. You just need some rest—"

He never finished the sentence. His chest and head were suddenly obscured by a cloud of blood and gore, gunfire shattering the uncomfortable silence, plowing through the hallway like a rampaging rhinoceros.

Sofia stumbled back into the stretchers, screaming as her coworker smashed into the doorjamb, half his head caved in by the savage sledgehammer impacts of assault rifle fire. She lunged forward, trying to catch him, as if there were possibly some hope that a human being could take so much damage and still somehow be alive. She couldn't hold him up. He was a heavy, limp thing, a formless blob spilling and pouring over her arms and tumbling to the floor no matter how much she tried to grab on.

Sofia looked up and saw Gerda, still out in the hall, her eyes staring up at the ceiling, her chest peppered with apple-sized splotches of red on her scrubs. But Gerda's green eyes were bulging, her forehead literally dented an inch deep, a tiny red hole in the bottom of the crater in her face.

It was the camp all over again.

Sofia looked for another exit, knowing that if she went out into the hall, she'd end up as shredded meat. Charles and Gerda had granted her a reprieve with their deaths, and she had to get out, to warn people.

It was them.

Sofia wasn't fighting her fears, her paranoia anymore. If it was the dark men who came to slaughter the families of suspected terrorists, then they were coming after her because they knew she would willingly testify.

She threw herself across a pair of tables, feeling the lumps of flesh under bloodied linens shift beneath her. On hands and knees she crawled frantically, charging toward the window on the far side of the storage room turned morgue. Sofia hated herself as she looked back, watching the dead girl she tried to help, half spilled off her gurney, brown eyes fallen open, staring with glassy indifference toward her.

Guilt wrapped around her throat with strangling strength, but she tore away from the eye contact with the dead, slamming her palm into the base of the window to force it open. It stopped her cold. Screams and gunfire ripped horribly through the building behind her. She slapped the window frame a second time, and it budged a quarter of an inch.

"Open, dammit," she cursed.

The gunfire went silent as she punched the window frame again. It was the same hand she'd smashed over and over again into the gurney handle, and each strike sent fiery pain shooting up her arm. Blood was pouring freely from split skin, but Sofia finally got the window levered open wide enough to squeeze through.

Something crashed behind her and Sofia froze. She looked over her shoulder and saw a sad-faced man, overturning stretchers, dumping corpses to the floor. She recognized his face from the night of slaughter that had sent her halfway across a continent to escape retribution.

Her muscles were seemingly paralyzed, though some part of her mind recognized that she was actually moving—he was simply moving faster. Fear sent her adrenaline level skyrocketing, and time felt as if it were slowing down.

It gave her a chance to feel like she could live longer as the gun in the murderer's hand rose slowly toward her. Sofia's hand was through the window. She was in midfall to the ground outside.

A flash of light emitted from the barrel, though there was no loud crack of a gunshot.

Time suddenly snapped back to normal as her head was driven back, crashing into the half-opened window. Glass shattered and cleaved through her scalp, turning her blond locks to a ruddy crimson.

The next shot that Steiner pumped into Sofia DeLarroque's face didn't bounce obliquely along the curved bone of her skull. This .22 slug hit dead on, penetrating the fragile shell of her temple, tearing deep into the UN worker's brain.

She was alive, technically, even as her brain cells were spun into a frothy soup by the bouncing bullet. Her heart still beat, and she still had reflexes that crashed her completely through the opened window. The frame snagged her, holding her as muscles flinched, making Sofia's corpse twitch and twist.

Steiner walked up to the dying woman, looking her up and down. Blue eyes, the color of a tropical sea, glimmered, staring into a cloudless sky, lips moving wordlessly.

"Go to sleep, girl," Steiner said, pulling the trigger on the Beretta twice more.

The Israeli unscrewed the sound suppressor from his pistol and stowed both pieces in his gear.

This wasn't over, the assassin knew.

Where it would stop was anyone's guess.

2

Hal Brognola chewed into his unlit cigar so hard he felt his teeth ache, as the voice on the other end of the phone line spoke.

"I'm going on a hunting trip, Hal."

"Dammit, Striker," Brognola spoke up. The handset was plugged into a hardline at Stony Man Farm, a top secret facility in the Blue Ridge Mountains of Virginia. Even with the latest encryption hardware and software protecting the call, years of experience had taught him that nothing was one hundred percent secure, and even after all this time, he was not in the habit of talking openly on the phone with the man whose voice he knew intimately.

Experience had also taught Brognola something about the man he called Striker. Once he made up his mind to accomplish a goal, nothing would stop him.

"Dammit, Striker," Brognola repeated, "I think I know what you're looking at."

"You think," came the reply. There was no mockery or challenge in his tone. Brognola and Striker were friends who respected each other too much to play word games. "There's a big wide world out there, Hal. A world that needs me to act between the jobs you have for me."

Brognola grunted. He tasted the buds of tobacco squeezed

from the crushed cigar between his teeth and set it down on an ash tray. Spitting residue from the tip of his tongue, he looked at the desktop full of news clippings and intelligence reports that made up the hell that was tearing through the world at that very moment.

It was the same crap, just different names. Terrorists. Mobsters. Drug dealers. Murderers. Conspiracies. Threats ranging from the schoolyard to the ivory towers of governments and corporations. This was the world that Brognola looked at every day, a wall of mourning and misery that he had to pick and choose from, and apply the powerful resources of America's most elite covert action organization against.

To have Striker, one of Stony Man's most important allies...

That was the truth about their arrangement, Brognola reminded himself.

Mack Samuel Bolan, the Executioner, wasn't an employee. He wasn't a recruit. He wasn't a member of Stony Man Farm. The Executioner was the cat who walked by himself. He chose whether to go along with the soldiers of Able Team or Phoenix Force when they needed an extra hand. And he chose when to discharge his duties elsewhere.

The career of the big soldier wasn't one defined by pay, or orders. It was entirely personal. It had started with destroying major chunks of the criminal organization that drove his family to its death. It moved up to battling terrorists, and then to the Executioner's realization that there was more that needed to be done than what was sanctioned by any pencil-pushing politician or even Brognola himself.

"I'm sorry. Thanks for letting us know that you've got other pots cooking," the big Fed said. His cheeks burned, even though he knew Bolan would forgive him.

"If it's any consolation, you could be right about who I might be doing," Bolan said.

"I'm betting it's Chaman," Brognola said, pulling the report of an attack on a relief hospital setup near a refugee camp in Afghanistan.

"Remind me to keep you away from Las Vegas," Bolan said.

A chuckle relieved the pressure in Brognola's gut. "I dunno. I don't remember having much time to place bets any time we've been to Vegas. Besides, I'd be much more interested in catching one of the shows."

"Well, that's one thing Vegas and Chaman will have in common," the Executioner said.

Brognola chuckled. "You've always been known for your tiger impersonation."

"Yeah. But when I put my teeth into someone's neck, I intend to take their head off," Bolan said.

MACK BOLAN WENT to Afghanistan in answer to the murders of UN relief workers, but he went not to bury them, but to insure that no one else would fall. The soldier's duty he undertook didn't have room for feelings of hatred and revenge.

He needed assistance, and while the cyberteam he usually relied upon at Stony Man Farm might have proved helpful anywhere else, in the technological wasteland of Afghanistan, Internet evidence of the suspected Taliban perpetrators was scarce.

That meant that the Executioner was going to have to go hunting the old-fashioned way. Electronics only went so far, but human eyes and ears, and trusted old friends, could reach further and deeper than anything. When the world was still in a cold, cold war, Bolan had been to Afghanistan often and had built up a network of allies, warriors among the *mujahideen,* the first and finest of whom was Tarik Khan, an old ally from the very last days that Bolan had been known as Colonel John Phoenix.

Aleser Khan looked every bit the younger version of his Uncle Tarik, and though he didn't know Bolan personally, the two men knew each other by reputation. The young leader accepted the soldier into his camp as if he were a long lost cousin, and listened to the Executioner's reasons for being there. Aleser's dark brown eyes flashed with outrage, not at his presence, but at the need for the Executioner's presence. His long black hair flowed like the mane of the lion he was named after.

"My uncle and my cousin owe you their lives, Al-Askari. It matters not which name you travel under. You will always have the best Aleser Khan can provide you, in men or arms," the young *mujahideen* leader told him. "Especially when it comes to righting the wrongs done by those who claim to be our countrymen."

"Thank you." Bolan accepted, glad at Aleser's facility with English. While the soldier knew enough Arabic to help him get around most of the Middle East, the Dahri dialect wasn't one he was as skilled with. "I know that the men of the Taliban are no sons of this land, just another conquering army in a long line," he said.

"That they succeeded so well leaves the taste of ashes in my mouth, Colonel," Aleser stated. "We would hunt them down ourselves, but your military commanders tell us that it is their job to insure the peace."

Bolan frowned. "They mean well, but sometimes they tie the wrong hands. Mine, however, are free."

"Tarik Khan spoke of your willingness to step outside the laws thrown in your path. What others consider walls, you step over as scratches in the dirt," Aleser stated. "Ask what you will, and I shall give you anything."

Bolan was already well-armed, thanks to the generosity of Khan. He didn't want to risk the lives of any others in his crusade. All Bolan needed, and asked for, was information—a handle on his enemy so he could work his way up the chain of command. Aleser responded totally. Though disappointed the request was so simple, and that he would do no more than act as a pointer, the Afghan warrior not only gave Bolan a handle, but a road map of potential Taliban targets, from desert training camps untouched by the U.S. military to urban cells nestled in towns, hiding under the noses of their enemy.

"It is the same information I have given many in your government," Aleser said, dejectedly.

"Let me guess. Nobody acted on any of it," Bolan replied.

Aleser shook his head, a deep melancholy in his leonine eyes. "And now, unarmed healers and caregivers lay dead at their hands. Only say the word, Colonel, and I shall assemble fifty of my best men, and we shall descend upon them and slay them all."

"It's tempting," Bolan stated, "and I am honored by your offer. I cannot risk, however, our forces mistaking you for the enemy. If you are armed for war, and lurking around our area of control..."

Aleser nodded.

"I look like one of them, at least. And one man can disappear more easily than fifty," Bolan explained.

"Then if you wish stealth and a low profile, you will need more than one man."

"I cannot—" Bolan began.

"You cannot speak our dialects fluently. You come seeking information, and you will undoubtedly come across more in your quest," Aleser replied. "My younger brother, Laith, he speaks English as well as I do, as well as half a dozen local dialects. He moves like a hunting cat, is good with a gun, but will follow orders."

"Are you sure?" Bolan asked. "I've been assigned young bucks in the past."

Aleser smiled and put a reassuring hand on Bolan's shoulder. "Laith's enthusiasm has been long since tempered. The wilderness does not suffer many fools."

Aleser gestured toward the newcomer entering the tent, a young man just inches short of six feet, with short, curly black hair and light brown eyes that flickered golden with the reflected lamplight. He looked out of place in the Afghan camp, and for a moment, Bolan wasn't sure if it was one of the *mujahideen,* or perhaps a Green Beret assigned to the area.

The newcomer was dressed not in the traditional robes of an Afghan warrior, but in a green coverall that Bolan recognized as a Nomex jumpsuit, used by American pilots and Special Forces soldiers alike. Over the flight suit was a black vest festooned with tool and magazine pouches. One of the pouches had been improvised into a holster for a handgun. While the outfit was relatively clean, Bolan saw signs that this wasn't original GI issue for the young man.

The jumpsuit showed wear and tear, weathering except for patches just below the youth's elbow and kneepads. The previous owner, having worn similar joint protection, kept those parts of the garment looking newer. The cuffs on his wrists were turned in, and the young Afghan wore no gloves, a mainstay of U.S. operators in either full or fingerless form for the past decade. The final clue was the lack of shooting glasses.

Bolan aside, no active American special operations trooper

as young as this man would be caught without a set of protective eyewear.

Laith Khan looked Bolan over, evaluating him, but not challenging. Apparently the Executioner met the young man's standards of approval, because Laith took a step forward and extended his hand. "It is a pleasure to meet the man who saved my cousin and my uncle."

"I am honored by the hospitality of your tribe," Bolan answered, shaking hands. The kid's grip was strong, and his fingers not quite so callused as his older brother's. The almost golden eyes held his stare for a moment, then the young man stepped back, hands at his sides, head tilted just slightly, watching Bolan studiously. His body language was calm and observant, even more so than Aleser. While Aleser did his best to show the strength and power of a commander, Laith staked no claims of dominance. Bolan looked slyly to Aleser.

"You anticipated me?" he asked.

Aleser nodded. "You were regarded as a wise and skilled man. Such wisdom is written that a man has to know his limitations, and the wisest of such men is truly intimate with his limitations and accepts them."

Bolan caught Laith's slight smile. His shoulders straightened and he untilted his head. It was the first show of pride he'd noted in the younger Khan, and it was a subtle one.

"Come on, Laith. It's time to go hunting," Bolan said.

ROBERT WESLEY CROUCHED behind the wreckage of the burned-out Volkswagen, casting a nervous glance back at the woman in fatigues he was supposedly guarding. From everything he'd seen of Theresa Rosenberg, she needed a bodyguard like a pit bull needed a switchblade.

It wasn't that she was particularly rough or hard around the edges. She had a flinty gaze, but that was due to alertness, and her round face was soft and attractive, with full lips. Staff Sergeant Welsey couldn't explain it. While she didn't look anything like a soldier, she looked exactly like some of the best soldiers he'd ever met as a Special Forces A-Team member. Not in appearance, but the way she moved, the way her eyes were always in motion, never settling on any one thing.

Theresa Rosenberg had the warrior mentality, and Wesley doubted she could have gained it easily. You got that kind of alertness only by having walked through the valley of the shadow of death, and proving yourself one bad mother.

Wesley idly wondered if you could refer to a woman that way, but then movement outside the collection of battered buildings drew him back into the moment. He had been silently complimenting the Israeli woman on her ability to be one with her surroundings, and he nearly let his attention wander fatally.

"Couple more guards, side one, moving toward side four," Staff Sergeant Luis Montenegro spoke up through their LASH radio set. The terminology was developed by the LAPD long ago, side one being the front, and turning in a clockwise manner. In a situation where north and south were confusing, people could determine which side was "front." And front was always the place to start.

"We see it," Rosenberg whispered. She slid prone, resting on her elbows. The stock of her M-4 carbine pressed her left cheek. Only now did Wesley realize that she was a southpaw.

Odd details bubbled to the surface when the adrenaline hit the bloodstream, and Wesley remembered the term called tache-psyche syndrome. In some instances, it meant that time seemingly slowed down for people. In others, people could count the ridges on the front sights of their pistols. At its most dangerous, peripheral vision blacked out and noises and speech sounded like they were trying to pierce pillows stuffed over the ears.

The Green Beret took a few deep breaths, oxygenating his blood. His fingers tingled despite the fact that he had them crushed down hard on the pistol grip and forearm of his Special Operations Modification M-4 carbine. The SOPMOD was outfitted with all kinds of things to make a firefight easier, from big holographic dot sights, recoil-reducing muzzle brakes and forearm pistol grips to flashlights, lasers and infrared illuminators. Wesley's rifle was painted in desert camouflage patterns.

The Israeli woman, on the other hand, had her carbine wrapped with burlap and twine. Sand and dust caked into the weave of the heavy cloth, making it better camouflaged than the sleek lines of the heavily customized rifle Wesley had. Rosenberg's only concession to "modern" technology was an Aimpoint sight.

"They haven't noticed us, yet," she said finally. She spoke without any hint of an Israeli accent.

"Only a matter of time," Wesley answered. "Hush the chatter."

She glanced over at him, then gave him a wink, her emerald green eyes twinkling. She took a breath to speak, then paused, thinking better of it, and just nodded.

Wesley loosened his grip on the SOPMOD, laying it down gently. Through binoculars, he scanned the men walking around the corner. They looked woozy and were leaning against each other. One passed the other a pipe, and he took a deep hit from it, holding in his breath for a long time before streaming white smoke out of his nostrils. Wesley shook his head and swept the binoculars over to the front of one home.

Amber firelight spilled through the portal, backlighting two men standing out front. One shook his head with the same disbelief Wesley had at the two pipe smokers.

The Green Beret took these two men seriously. The AK-47s they held were all business, and at only one hundred yards out, he was well within range of those deadly, efficient man killers. Too many American soldiers, from Vietnam to the streets of Tikrit had learned how dangerous those weapons were, even in the hands of rag tag thugs.

According to Rosenberg, these weren't just ragtag thugs. They had connections with a Middle Eastern group and had received training, weaponry and funding. Wesley had asked who. He was in intelligence and operations, after all. Knowing who they'd be up against could be vital, life-saving information. Rosenberg kept those cards close to her vest. She said it was suspected that they might be Syrians. Rich, powerful, well-armed and willing to share all kinds of training…

"We have movement coming in from side four," Montenegro's voice whispered over the LASH. "Two figures."

Wesley brought his binoculars back to the two pipe smokers. Hashish, heroin or marijuana, he didn't know what the pair was smoking, but they were not so buzzed as to fail to react to a pair of shadows rising from the scrub brush that reclaimed shattered town roads. As the Green Beret was about to take action, he watched the two smokers stiffen, jerking in response to silent, but lethal impacts. For a moment, he could have sworn he'd seen the flicker of reflected steel and the red-pencil flare of a suppressed handgun's muzzle-flash. The hashed-up thugs collapsed into lifeless piles of limbs and robes. As quickly as the shadows had appeared, they were atop the dead men.

The smaller man wrenched something wicked, curved and

metallic from one corpse while the other covered him with a large pistol, a suppressor on the muzzle.

"Are they friendlies?" Montenegro asked. Perched atop the M240 light machine gun, even with the barrel shaped and steel-drum tough ECLAN scope atop it, he was watching all the action from the cheap seats.

Wesley glanced at Rosenberg, whose mouth gaped with surprise. Then she smirked.

"Get ready to watch a show," she whispered.

MACK BOLAN WAS IMPRESSED with Laith Khan's stealth and skill with a thrown blade, but he didn't let it get in the way of going about the grim and silent business of bringing death and getting prisoners. Laith's skills simply reinforced the Executioner's confidence that Aleser had given him a reliable backup.

They slipped quickly around the corner and Bolan put away his pistol, exchanging it for the head weapon for this assault. Entering Afghanistan with his faithful signature weapons was a task that would have required more official support than the Executioner wanted for this mission. He'd opted for a low profile, at least in terms of ties to the West. A diplomatic pouch for his Beretta and Desert Eagle were out of the question, and a war bag full of larger weapons, grenades and ammunition was impossible.

Instead, Bolan set down with nothing more than his Applegate-Fairbairn folding knife, a .32-caliber Beretta Tomcat hidden inside the guts of a camera and plenty of spending money to give to the Peshwar gun dealers in Pakistan.

Bolan's silenced pistol was a NORINCO NP228, a Chinese knockoff of the 9 mm SIG-Saur P-228 autoloader. He also managed to get a Taurus Model 44 with a 6.5-inch barrel and a 6-shot capacity. It didn't reload as fast or hold as many shots as his Desert Eagle, but it was accurate, and more importantly, it was with him.

The head weapon was a severely cutdown version of the AK-47 called the Zastava M-92. It was chambered for a rifle round, the 7.62 mm COMBLOC, and was no larger than most submachine guns. It gave Bolan an incredible power advantage in a small package. While recoil didn't bother Bolan, the muzzle-flash of such a short-barrel rifle would give away his position, so the only modification was a segment of PVC pipe over the muzzle that provided room for the superhot, flaming gases to disperse while only adding minimal length to the agile little gun.

Bolan was counting on speed and audacity to get his work done. The Zastava was suited for such action. He stuffed the muzzle through the canvas curtains over the doorway, using it as a spear to cleave his way into the firelit room. Men rose, scrambling and crying out at the sight of the Executioner, tall and fearsome with his hands and face smeared black with grease paint, clad head to toe in black clothing and black military gear.

"On the ground now!" he shouted in Arabic, repeating the sharp command that Laith had taught him.

Some dropped at the sound of his bellowing voice, but others weren't buying orders, even from Death himself.

One robed thug was scrambling for a rifle in the corner, but a more immediate threat was a second man, pulling his knife and charging, letting out a shrill scream of challenge. Bolan swung his weapon around and stroked the trigger. A blistering salvo of slugs smashed into the attacker, ripping him from crotch to beard, sending him flying backward. In the enclosed space, the roar of the short rifle was staggering.

The guy reaching for the rifle stopped short at the thunderstorm that signaled the gore-splashed demise of his comrade, shock widening his eyes. Bolan tracked the PVC-piped muzzle of the Zastava around to catch the gunner, but the Taliban rifleman got his weapon and dived into the next room as bullets smashed the wall where he had been moments before.

"Laith, keep these guys honest," Bolan shouted, pointing to the prisoners.

There was a moment of conflict in the younger man's face as he watched the doorway through which Bolan's quarry disappeared. The Executioner respected that the Afghan fighter acknowledged his responsibilities over glory. There still was the danger that the moment Bolan left the room, his presence would no longer cow the trembling Taliban supporters facedown on the floor.

Bolan didn't envy Laith's task should a melee take place. He plunged through the doorway, hit a shoulder roll and kept tight to the ground. His low-down approach kept him alive to fight another day as not one but three muzzle-flashes lit up the hallway, bullets chewing into the door frame as he tumbled past it. Throwing himself on his stomach, the Executioner brought up his rifle and triggered off four short bursts, sweeping the darkness where he remembered the muzzle flashes originating.

Only one cry of agony answered Bolan's hellstorm of fire. The soldier cursed, knowing that he was in the open, his position given away by the harsh flare of his rifle's muzzle, and flat on his belly with his hands full. A shadow swung around the corner, and wild gunfire ripped all along the hallway, still at chest height as the enemy muzzle-flash bobbed up and down as if to the beat of some macabre sing-along. With a hard shove, Bolan pushed himself to one side in time to avoid a blast of slugs that chewed along the floor he was slumped on. He abandoned his rifle and watched as impacts propelled the weapon down the hall.

Bolan's hand had dropped to his thigh, grabbing for the holstered .44 Magnum Taurus when, over the ringing in his ears, he heard the metallic thunk of a canister bouncing off wood. Looking up, he saw the unmistakable shape of a fragmentation grenade thumping toward him.

3

The sound of AK-47s going off was Rosenberg's signal to get up and charge toward the squat hovel that the Taliban suspects had chosen to call home. She recognized one of the two men making the assault on the thugs inside, and even though she had watched him battle a mine complex full of heavily armed killers, she couldn't sit idly by and watch him risk a chestful of rifle fire in conflict with a room full of hashed-up terrorists.

On her heels Sergeant Wesley was grunting and huffing as he tried to match his long strides with her short, pumping legs. Over her LASH headset, she listened to Montenegro shouting about rules of engagement and Captain Blake.

There was a time to play by the rules, she thought.

And there was a time to play it like the man she knew as Striker.

Usually, that time came the moment the big mystery soldier strode onto the scene, making his presence felt like a herd of bison crashing across a plain.

A firefight was blazing inside, but nobody was making a break for it. She reached the front in time to see a figure fly backward out the door, his rifle blazing as the canvas draping the entrance fluttered closed. She struck the wall beneath the window, crouching. She watched as Wesley, not even pausing, bent and scooped up the lithe young form with the rifle and dragged him away from the doorway in time to avoid a hail of gunfire punching through the curtains.

"What?" she heard the fighter say as he realized he was being handled like a rag doll.

The thunderous sound of gunshots filled the air from the other side of the opening. A heartbeat later, a tall lean figure burst through the curtain, pistols in each hand. The compression wave and its subsequent debris cloud chased the diving form of the man as he somersaulted away from the doorway.

He came up, almost like a snake in his speed and agility, leveling two long-barreled guns at her, but only for a heartbeat before raising the muzzles skyward.

"I figure at least two gunners are making a break for it out the back," he said. "We need someone to interrogate in case nobody survived the explosion."

Rosenberg watched him in amazement for a moment, then pressed her throat mike tighter to her voice box. "Sergeant Montenegro, we need suppression fire. No fatalities."

The Special Forces weapons officer had quit complaining about rules of engagement and answered with a terse "Affirmative."

The night lit up as in the distance, Montenegro's Squad Automatic Weapon spewed a line of heavy fire across the darkness. Rosenberg looked back and saw that the warrior was gone, vanished like a shadow.

"Go get 'em Striker," she whispered.

MACK BOLAN'S EYES FOCUSED on the grenade in an instant, the bouncing hellbomb grabbing his attention in an almost fatal stranglehold.

Almost.

The grenade's pull ring and spoon were still locked in place, despite the rolling jumps it was making toward him. Bolan had used a similar tactic many times in the past, throwing a grenade with the pin still in it to flush out an enemy into shooting range.

Instead, Bolan held his ground. He fisted the Taurus as he got up from all fours, and lowered his hand to scoop the RPG-1 grenade as it came to him. Throwing himself against the near wall, he thumbed the pin loose from the miniblaster and launched it back where it came from.

Gunfire erupted wildly in the main room, and the Executioner caught a glimpse of Laith in full retreat, blasting away. His voice, almost smothered by the roar of his rifle blazing in full fury, was shouting warnings. The body of one Taliban supporter jerked violently under a salvo of savage strikes, fatal impacts driving the dead man's corpse into two of his allies.

The Executioner straight-armed the Taurus. He drew the NP228 with his free hand and pumped the triggers of both handguns to lay down a wall of bullets that crashed into the disorganized gunmen while their backs were still to him. He plunged through the room, the mighty .44 Magnum empty but still clicking as he pulled the trigger, the 9 mm weapon still spitting its quiet payloads of death. He was out the door just as the grenade went off. The fatal blast radius of the grenade was ten yards, and Bolan wasn't sticking around to be sliced to ribbons by hurtling shrapnel.

The whole event took moments, and Bolan dived into a shoulder roll, tumbling so as to reverse himself and not present his back to the enemies he knew were behind him.

What he didn't expect was the sight of two soldiers out front. A lightning quick assessment showed one as a U.S. special operations trooper of some sort, and the other was a woman, dressed to keep up with the American soldier. As he raised the muzzles of both pistols to defuse any thought of a standoff, he made out the face. Even partially shaded by her helmet, he picked up some recognizable features, though it was too dark for him to be certain. His gut instinct told him that she was a friend, and he went with it.

"I figure at least two gunners making a break for it out the back," he told her. "We need someone to interrogate in case nobody survived the explosion."

She touched her throat mike, and as he heard her voice, he confirmed who she was.

Tera Geren, a gutsy Israeli agent Bolan had worked with before.

He didn't stick around to hear what she was saying, and he guessed that the machine gun fire in the distance was more American special operations ordinance, a SAW by the sound of it.

Long legs eating up the ground in effortless strides, Bolan swung around the building and spotted a quartet of men racing in the distance. They dropped to the ground, cowering from the sizzling onslaught of autofire raking all around them, but the gunner wasn't firing for effect. Bolan paused, fed a fresh speedloader into the Taurus, slapped a fresh clip into the NP228, then continued his charge.

The SAW fire let up, and the Taliban lackeys slowly got to their feet, looking to where the onslaught came from, firing wildly from their AKs. Marksmanship was an illusory skill that the gunmen thought they possessed, and having fully automatic weapons instilled in them the delusion that they didn't have to aim. Whoever the gunner was, he was safe. The pathetic riflery skill of the Taliban killers was barely enough to spray the broadside of a street cafe. Against real soldiers who took cover, conserved ammo, and watched the front sight, they were standing sacks of meat ready to be plucked by a short burst.

The distraction of the Taliban fighters bought the Executioner a few seconds, enough time to close to hand-to-hand range. With a savage snap, he hammered the butt of the Brazilian revolver hard across the jaw of the first man he ran into. The punch, backed by four pounds of stainless steel, felled the thug.

The second man was turning, but not nearly fast enough to avoid Bolan's boot rocketing into his groin. The mercenary for the former occupational government folded over, head dropping to where the Executioner slashed his elbow down mercilessly like his namesake's ubiquitous ax.

Two down, one to go, and Mack Bolan's free rein over his enemies ended.

Too close to bring up his rifle and fire, the last man merely swung the barrel hard at the Executioner. The front sight hooked Bolan's wrist, wrenching the revolver from his grasp. Bolan brought his NP228 around to shoot the guy and be done with him, but the fighter wasn't finished swinging. The pistol grip of the AK crashed off Bolan's cheek and left his head reeling.

Bolan dropped back, dazed. The rifle slashed out again. The soldier brought up his left hand to block the next chop and felt his forearm go numb. The Chinese pistol sailed from his grasp.

The Executioner wasn't standing still. He kicked the guy in the knee, a dead center blow struck with his steel-toed combat boots. With a cry, the rifleman staggered, letting go of his weapon and windmilling his arms to maintain his balance. Bolan didn't allow him any mercy, launching two right jabs with pistonlike speed. The Taliban fighter's nose exploded, rivers of blood streaming down into his mustache and beard. Another step forward, and Bolan folded his opponent over his knee. A hammering fist dropped savagely on the back of the thug's head and with a savage twist, Bolan hurled the half-conscious man over his hip.

"Give up," Bolan said, picking up the sand-covered .44 Magnum pistol. He aimed the tunnellike barrel at the militiaman's nose.

Eyes wide, the man muttered what sounded like gibberish to Bolan's ears, and passed out.

Bolan lowered the Taurus, then brought his fingers to his swollen cheek, tears welling in his eyes from the sting.

"Striker!" he heard Tera Geren shout. He looked up and saw her running toward him alongside Laith and two big guys in nomex jumpsuits and boonie hats.

"That's Colonel Brandon Stone," Bolan told her.

Geren paused, looking at her allies, then presented her hand. "Theresa Rosenberg."

Bolan nodded. "And your friends?"

"Staff Sergeants Wesley and Montenegro," Geren answered. "U.S. Special Forces."

"Green Berets?" Laith asked.

"Yeah," Wesley said apprehensively, while Montenegro simply nodded. "You don't dress like a local."

"To prevent friendly fire, soldier," Bolan explained. "He's my guide."

"Uh-huh," Wesley said. "And what's he guiding you to?"

"All the hottest tourist traps on the map," Bolan said.

"Tourist traps?" Laith asked. "Oh, Colonel Stone, I'm sorry. I thought you said terrorist traps." He shook his head. "English is only my second language."

Bolan rested a hand on Laith's shoulder. "It was an honest mistake, though I can see now why you suggested bringing a .44 Magnum along to pick up girls."

Laith shrugged and turned to face the others. "Well, if you don't mind, we'll be off."

Bolan saw Geren struggling to control her laughter, but the Special Forces sergeants weren't buying it. "We're taking these men for interrogation," Wesley said, pointing to the surviving Taliban fighters.

"We were supposed to be snooping and pooping on these creeps," he explained. "You interfered with that."

"And what are you doing here?" Bolan asked Geren.

"Protecting truth, justice and a really good kosher pickle," she replied.

Yeah, Bolan thought. Tera Geren was still a red-hot firecracker.

"Thanks for the update," Bolan said.

"Let's not waste a valuable intelligence opportunity," Geren told Wesley. "We've captured people who might lead us to the UN hit."

"You're working this too?" Bolan asked.

Geren glanced up at him. "We have to talk, Colonel," she said stiffly.

Bolan remained silent, answering with only a nod. The atmosphere drained of whatever relief he'd felt at the sight of a familiar ally.

He dismissed his disappointment at being at cross-purposes with Geren. It was an occupational hazard that he'd faced before, all too often. When working with someone who was loyal to and spilled blood for the safety of the land of her birth, there was always the possibility that the people in the field could end up flipping from friends to enemies.

And even if they weren't enemies, they'd still end up doing their own thing.

A situation like that could get people killed.

MARID HAYTHAM KNEW the woman on sight. She was a member of the Israel's secret police—one of the accursed enemies who hunted down his allies relentlessly. She was good, but she usually worked alone, almost as if she were a sacrificial lamb no one wanted to be associated with. Some wondered if it was because she was a woman who dared to take on the duties of a man, but Haytham knew better.

Women were present in all levels of Israel's military. The country was in such a besieged state that women's liberation was a nonissue, even in the 1950s. If you had two arms and two legs, you were able to fight for your country.

Tera Geren was not very tall, but she had a robust build, probably padded out by the body armor she wore. Still, it presented her as someone substantial.

Haytham was tempted to raise his AK-47, rest the barrel on the door of his car and hold down the trigger, stitching her from crotch to throat, but for once, he was reluctant to take out his fury on a known Jewish agent.

For one part, she had a reputation of not being a hard case who targeted bystanders. Because she worked as a lone wolf, she spent a lot of time alone among Palestinian and non-Palestinian Arabs who lived in Israel. Both groups seemed to consider her, grudgingly, as someone who was sympathetic to their desires to live in peace on land that they owned. She came down hard only on enemies who had killed, and who could fight back.

For the second part, he and his team were in Afghanistan to look for the same men she was seeking.

It was one thing for Israel to launch rockets into Palestinian towns. It was another for them to send in men to slaughter the children and wives of freedom fighters as if they were no more than dogs.

Haytham had his orders.

The men who were responsible for the deaths in the Shafeeq Refugee camp had to die. The blood of brothers, sisters, wives, sons, daughters, nieces and nephews had been spilled by merciless fusillades of bullets. The camp of compassion and tenderness had been turned into an abbatoir by cowardly men who had swooped down on the unarmed, the sick and the starving.

Haytham wanted to pull the trigger and wipe out the Jewish woman, but he knew that for now, she was an ally in that she would have a better chance of tracking down the killers. She had contacts, she knew about hideouts and she would be relentless, if the orders that were intercepted were true.

Haytham frowned.

He hated to admit that the Mossad would actually be interested in hunting down the men he had been ordered to kill. It meant that there were Jews who were actually interested in justice, even for the families of their sworn enemies.

It happened every so often—these moments of doubt. In the young fighter his superiors saw a powerful warrior ready to burst free, but one who was not willing to fight recklessly in the street. Instead of supervising a suicide bombing, he was more likely to be involved in direct conflict with armed Israeli troops.

Hamas needed all types of fighters. As long as Haytham's dedication was unflinching when it came to facing enemy soldiers, then he had a task.

He was seeking justice against a band of savage killers.

He watched as others assembled around Geren. American soldiers, heavily armed and capable of wiping him out if they detected him, flanked her. They kept the muzzles of their rifles aimed at the ground, but their eyes swept the street as others came out to greet them. Two more men, one an Afghan, the other a tall, lean, grim soldier dressed in black, joined Geren and the American Special Forces troops.

On the street, there were easily a dozen people, all but Geren, the tall wraith in black and the Afghan were toting rifles and handguns. Whatever opportunity Haytham had had to strike a blow against the Israelis and America was gone. Twelve bodies were too many even for the 30-round magazine of an AK-47 on full-auto. He'd cause at least one or two deaths, and several injuries, but the others would dive for cover.

And with that many guns present, Haytham would never have the opportunity to reload.

In a way, the young eagle was relieved.

With temptation cut off, he had retained his window of opportunity. The woman would still be able to provide him with intelligence regarding the killers at Shafeeq.

He hunkered down, watching and waiting.

SPECIAL FORCES CAPTAIN Jason Blake watched as Wesley and Montenegro returned from their surveillance mission with Theresa Rosenberg and the newcomers in tow.

"Care to explain yourself?" Blake asked as the two intruders reported to him. He rose, as a sign of respect for the alleged "Colonel Stone's" rank, but he restrained a salute. Salutes were more appropriate for safe Army bases stateside. Out in the real shit, such acknowledgment of rank could mean the difference between observation and a sniper's bullet.

"Not beating around the bush, are you?" Bolan asked.

"I'm waiting for an explanation why a full-bird colonel is running around the desert picking fights with former Taliban enforcers, without alerting me."

"I didn't know you had forces in the area," Bolan answered.

Blake shook his head. "No. Ignorance of my being here shouldn't be a case. Not if you're on the ball enough to have the little brother of one of our biggest *mujahideen* allies guiding him into a hot spot. At the very least, Aleser Khan should have let me know that someone was looking around in my backyard. Right, Laith?"

Bolan looked at Blake, then the young Afghan.

"My brother was sending word to you in the morning, Captain, so as not to disturb your sleep, nor to break curfew," Laith responded.

"And you broke curfew?" Blake asked in challenge.

Laith smiled confidently. "I was accompanied by an American military officer."

"An alleged American military officer," Blake growled. "This guy has ID, but he has no official paperwork or orders. I've radioed back to headquarters, and nobody's heard shit that some colonel was sweeping through on any form of inspection."

"The expression is 'need to know,'" Bolan stated.

"I do need to know. I'd like to know if an American, civilian or military, is running around killing locals and stirring up a hornet's nest of retaliation against my A-Team," Blake said angrily. "As it is, we had shots fired, and more than likely people saw American soldiers leaving natives, even if they were ex-Taliban, dead."

"I'm on an investigation. Asking permission would take time I really can't afford," Bolan replied.

"And I'm on a peacekeeping mission. Having some wild-assed nutrod running around on a vendetta is something I can't afford," Blake said. "I'm going to run some checks on who you are, Colonel Stone. Until then, your investigation is on hold. Hand over your weapons," Blake ordered.

Laith tensed, but the big American simply rested his hand on the young Afghan's shoulder. "No need to pick a fight with the U.S. Army, Laith."

"According to the law, I can keep my weapons as long as ammunition and gun are separated," Laith said. He pulled the magazines from his pistol and rifle and ejected the chambered rounds. A bullet bounced across Blake's desk, but the Afghan didn't bother picking it up. He simply slung the AK and glowered. "Unless you'd like to explain to my older brother why you had me arrested for following the letter of the agreement we made."

Blake clenched his jaw.

Laith took a deep breath, exhaling hard out flared nostrils.

"I was addressing Colonel Stone," Blake said, recovering his control of the situation. "And the next time you violate weapons policy in my camp, you will be thrown into the stockade for a very long stay."

Laith smirked in defiance, but Blake was satisfied he'd made his point. Controlling the young lion wasn't an easy task, but he was glad to have the youth mollified for the time being. It was the tall, rangy American who gave the Special Forces captain pause.

Even though Stone acquiesced to Blake's orders, he knew it was only lip service. The stranger no more intended to stay on a short leash and behave himself than Laith did. At least by confiscating the big man's guns, the captain had managed to slow him down, somewhat.

Blake watched the man unload his arsenal. The pile of weapons grew until finally, almost as an afterthought, a tiny little black, five-and-a-half-inch-long pocket pistol and three slender magazines were placed on the desk.

Blake chuckled. "No, really. I wanted all your guns." He wondered who this guy could be.

"Keep your knives," Blake said, picking up the little black pocket pistol. It was a .32-caliber Beretta Tomcat. Not much in terms of firepower compared to the monstrous, eleven-inch-long .44 Magnum Taurus it was placed beside, it was firepower that would mean the difference between being unarmed and helpless and having a fighting chance.

He handed over the Tomcat. "Take your Beretta too. I don't need to have you completely helpless. But the thing's so puny, you won't be assaulting armed gangs of Taliban reservists."

Bolan plucked the gun and his spare magazines from Blake's hand. "Thank you," he said and turned to leave.

"Colonel Stone," Blake spoke up.

The man in black stopped.

"Please wait to get clearance from me before you continue on. I don't want administrative shit sliding down my neck because some spook went and got himself killed on my watch."

Bolan glanced back at the Special Forces captain. "I'm not a spook. You're not going to catch flak. I'm not going to get myself killed. Have a good evening, Captain."

4

"If you want, you can borrow my AK," Laith offered as they walked away from Captain Blake's office.

"Thank you, Laith, but I'll make do until I can find a substitute," Bolan said.

"You had quite a bit of firepower. Did you have any more guns?" Laith asked.

"I kept a grenade in reserve, and didn't show him my backup folding knife, my impact Kerambit, or my garotte," Bolan told him. "I also have a spare barrel for the Beretta with an integral sound suppresser."

Laith nodded. "You plan ahead."

Bolan simply nodded.

They stopped as Tera Geren sidled up to them. "You boys have a nice visit with Captain Blake?"

"Absolutely charming," Bolan responded. "He lets you keep your weapons."

"Because I came and knelt at the altar of interagency protocol, big guy," Geren said. "You might try it some time. Works wonders." she grinned mischievously, then took a deep breath. "It's good to see you again."

Bolan nodded. He didn't want to acknowledge their closeness. He glanced over to Laith.

"I need someplace to do a little first aid, and maybe get some food in us," Bolan said, nodding to his Afghan companion. Geren looked at him, then nodded, her mischief replaced with a more serious look. "I also don't want to deal with spies, no matter how friendly or well-intentioned they are," Bolan said.

"I have a place I'm operating out of," Geren told him. "Two, actually. One that Blake knows about and has under surveillance."

"The other?" Bolan asked.

She smiled. "We'll go there when we have to."

Laith cast a nervous glance toward Bolan, who simply nodded to the younger man. "Not going to mind having me along, Ms. Rosenberg?" Laith asked.

Geren shrugged. "Why? Do you smoke cheap cigars or fart a lot?"

Laith relaxed. "No, ma'am."

"Oh, God, please don't call me ma'am. It makes me sound like your mother," she answered. "Call me Tera."

"Laith."

The woman looked to Bolan again, trying to keep her features subdued, but the surprise still crossed her face. Bolan figured that she didn't expect him to be close friends with Tarik Khan's nephew. "You really know how to make friends around here. Makes me wonder why Blake stripped you."

Suddenly, the Executioner caught a flash of movement in the corner of his eye. He lunged, one arm wrapping around Geren, his other hand clutching Laith's jumpsuit, all three of them crashing to the ground an instant before the night exploded with gunfire.

Assault rifles tore through the silence as Mack Bolan reached for the minuscule Beretta .32 in his pocket. He knew that even if it wasn't too late, its response would be too little.

ROBERT WESLEY HAD NEVER liked the fact that they were based out of an old office building in the small town of Ghiyath. He remembered the horror stories about embassies and Marine barracks. When he and the others had mentioned this to Blake, the response had been quick and forthcoming.

The four engineering experts in the A-Team, both the primary training and the secondary training sergeants, were put to work seeking the parts of the U-shaped office complex that were least vulnerable to a car bomb. Those areas would be the main HQ for the Special Forces.

Having a car roll up, park and detonate would be impossible. Trip wires, laser and standard wire would raise alerts from the alley behind the complex. A car bomb ramming into the main complex would be blunted by strategically placed cars, mined with high explosives. Anyone trying to ram through would upset the triggers on the blockades and end up with a premature detonation.

Blake took precautions. He didn't like being hung out to be target practice for dedicated psychopaths, either.

The captain, Wesley noted, was no-bullshit. He might have been hard, but he looked out for his men, and he looked out for the people he was assigned to protect.

Wesley watched as the pair they'd escorted back to the base left Blake's office, conversing quietly. He wanted to reserve judgment on the big man who had led a charge into a pit of terrorist thugs. Theresa Rosenberg seemed to like him, despite her efforts to seem aloof to the newcomer.

Then again, Theresa didn't trust Wesley, or the rest of the Special Forces A-Team with her real name. He didn't blame her; that was just the way the world of espionage and counterterrorism worked.

Wesley frowned as he watched her join Stone and Laith Khan once more.

Maybe it was a hint of jealousy on his part that kept Wesley from truly wanting to accept the black-haired, blue-eyed wraith who had entered the fray. Rosenberg acted more like a woman with Stone in a few moments than she had around the whole of the team for the week she'd been with them.

Wesley dismissed that. Getting jealous and workplace romances in combat situations were the construct of novelists and Hollywood scriptwriters. Bed-hopping games like that were a good way to insure a bullet in the back of the head, or a few moments of hesitation when death came charging down on you like an out of control bull. He would have liked life to be like a movie or a paperback novel, but the truth was, he had too much life to live, and too much job to do.

Wesley looked around. A car was waiting just outside the demarked zone in what the engineers considered to be a safe parking spot. An average-sized sedan parked at that point wouldn't cause more than a few broken windows if it detonated. If a truck parked inside the same radius, Blake would have his teams swoop on it, kill anyone sitting inside, and check the back for high explosives.

As it was, Wesley activated his LASH mike on the headquarters frequency. "We've got a gold-colored Peugeot parked a block away."

"I've been watching it for a couple hours. The guy inside is on stakeout, but other than smoking cigarettes, he's not causing us any harm," came the reply from Jerrud, the rooftop sniper.

"He look local?" Wesley asked.

Jerrud grunted. "Nope. First, he smokes way too much. That means he has money to burn on cigarettes. Plus, he dresses too Western."

"He hasn't noticed you, has he?" Wesley asked.

Jerrud chuckled. "I'm insulted."

"Pardon me—" Wesley started to joke.

Gunfire suddenly flashed. Rosenberg and the two newcomers were suddenly on the ground in a huddled lump, but only for a second as autofire raked the air where they once stood.

"We got hostiles!" Jerrud shouted.

"The car?" Wesley asked. Looking, he saw that the muzzle-flashes were far from the Peugeot, which had hit reverse hard. The muzzle of an AKM poked out the window, but it was aiming in the direction of the shooters. Gunfire flashed across the street in both directions, the fender and hood of the gold car suddenly peppered with impacts. The Peugeot spun out and tore off down the street.

Wesley shouldered his M-4, bringing the holographic scope on target to where he saw a couple rifle-toting gunners swinging their attention back toward Rosenberg and her companions. He milked the trigger for a short burst, but knew it was too quick, panic fire that didn't even slow down the enemy shooters. Around him, other rifles were opening up, and the street was turned into a battlezone.

Wesley felt a lump drop into his stomach as he watched the trio charge toward the enemy gunners.

THE EXECUTIONER WAS ON his feet in an instant. Even as one vehicle downrange was pouring on the steam in full reverse—opening fire on the gunners—he was taking advantage of time in slices that made the beat of a heart seem like an hour.

The .32-caliber Tomcat was in Bolan's big fist, but there was no way he was going to score fatal hits. The terrorists had picked their battlefield intelligently, well beyond accurate pistol range for most people, and behind cover solid enough to stop even the 5.56 mm rifle rounds of the Special Forces soldiers. With long, ground-eating strides, he pushed hard, knowing his only hope was to get inside the reach of his own weapon. Had he been armed with the Beretta 93-R machine pistol, or his .44 Magnum Desert Eagle, he might have chosen to fall back.

Unfortunately, he had a paranoid Special Forces A-team captain to thank for not having much firepower. He was aware of bodies racing behind him. Gunfire popped from his right, the chatter of an M-4 on semiauto. Tera Geren, not disarmed of her weapon, Bolan figured. To his left, he caught the sound of a magazine slamming into the well of another rifle. Laith was going to get into action with his M-92.

"Colonel!" came the cry. Bolan turned and paused, holding out his hands as the rifle was lobbed to him. Laith made the toss and reached for his handgun in the same fluid movement.

Bolan scooped the rifle out of the air, then turned his attention forward as rifle fire bellowed with increased fury. The Green Berets traded fire with the terrorists, but neither side was scoring a hit, as they were all entrenched behind solid cover.

One thug spotted Bolan and whipped his rifle around.

The Executioner didn't even have time to get a grip on Laith's rifle. He punched the .32 Beretta forward, opening fire and emptying out the 9-round payload of the little pistol. The rifleman jerked under multiple impacts, his face splashed with blood. Hardly the most powerful handgun on the battlefield, but the soldier remembered that long ago, some of his first shots fired in anger against the Mafia were from a .32. Size and power didn't matter anymore. They were within thirty yards of the enemy, and the fusillade, even fired on the run, was dead on target.

Bolan tossed aside the empty pistol and got both hands on

the Zastava. The muzzle exploded in a blast of flame and thunder. The steel-cored slugs smashed through the slab of plasterboard one terrorist was using for cover. His body jerked back violently, leaving a bloody smear on wall behind him. The corpse slid to the ground in a messy heap.

The Executioner held down the trigger for another short burst, a swarm of 7.62 mm slugs punching the skull of another Afghan rifleman. The gunner was still standing, triggering rounds blindly until a wave of 5.56 mm bullets from Tera Geren slashed open his chest and dropped him.

Cover fire from the Special Forces team members, except for the sniper who had the high ground, stopped. Bolan and his allies were dangerously close to the attackers, and there was a good chance that even the Green Berets would accidentally hit the three people. It didn't matter to the Executioner.

There were more gunners, about four strong, holed up on the other side of a half-fallen wall. Bolan's hand found the grenade he'd held in reserve and sent it sailing over the wall.

"Fire in the hole!" he called.

Bolan and companions hit the ground, gunfire raking the air over their heads now that the terrorists were no longer pinned down by enemy gunfire.

The chatter of autofire was cut off as Bolan's grenade ripped itself apart. The shock wave made the Executioner grunt. A severed arm and other debris landed in a heap right in front of his face.

Bolan looked up and saw one Taliban mercenary staggering. The terrorist struggled to stay upright, holding his weapon one-handed and leveling it at the big man in black.

Bolan fought to claw his M-92 from the pavement and get target acquisition, but the terrorist spun under multiple impacts. By the time his front sight was tracking the dying killer, he was already spilling over the half wall. Bolan glanced back, seeing a figure on the roof of the office complex shift, raising a fist in an "all stop" hand signal.

Bolan lowered the rifle, then looked back to Geren, who was holding the earpiece on her headset.

"They want us to stay put. Looking for more bad guys," Geren said. She quickly reloaded her rifle.

Laith skidded a spare magazine to Bolan.

The Executioner reloaded, keeping a wary eye on his surroundings.

"A little more excitement than you're used to?" Laith asked.

Bolan looked around. "No."

Laith wiped his brow. "The old curse bites again."

Bolan managed a smile. "May you live in interesting times."

CAPTAIN JASON BLAKE glowered at the man he knew as Colonel Brandon Stone. Stone had handed Laith Khan's rifle back to him nonchalantly after running a perimeter search for more bad guys.

Blake felt stretched like piano wire, and he was just as likely to cut into someone. He fought the urge to grind his teeth and tried to get some work done. "Good job. You're bleeding, though."

Stone touched his arm and came away with fresh glistening blood on his fingertips. A rifle round had to have clipped him. He wiped his fingers on his sleeve and shrugged it off. "I'll take care of it before it gets too bad. Right now, I want to check the terrorists."

"I have my team checking them. I have four intel-trained noncoms here, in case you don't know the set up of a—" Blake was sneering.

"I know the structure and training of a field deployed A-Team," Bolan said, cutting him off. "You don't have to treat me like an idiot."

"No, but I do have to treat you as an unknown quantity, Colonel Stone," Blake answered. "You might look good on paper, but anyone can fake a good cover. Until you tell me who you really are, I don't have to do fuck-all except treat you with skepticism and distrust."

There wasn't any indignation on Bolan's face. "Perfectly understandable, Captain," he said.

"And Laith, make that rifle compliant with curfew laws—now," Blake growled.

Laith ejected the clip and racked the bolt, all the while letting out a long, tired sigh. He stuffed the top round into a vent pocket and the magazine into an appropriate pouch. The young Afghan slung the rifle, then winked at Blake, pulled his pistol and did the same. "You forgot to warn me about my handgun."

Blake felt his cheeks grow hot.

"Don't worry. I remembered myself," Laith added.

Blake sighed and shook his head. "Find yourselves a place to bunk down for the night. You don't have to go home, but you're not sleeping here."

Laith shrugged. "Sounds like you've heard that order a few times before."

"Kid, you're starting to get on my nerves," Blake grunted.

"Then it's working," Laith responded. "Because you're getting on mine. Need I remind you whose nation you're in?"

Blake took a deep breath, remembering that as a member of the Army's Special Forces, he was a diplomat of American goodwill as well as a soldier. "No. But I can't break the rules for you. Otherwise, why have rules?"

"Why not try recognizing who your friends are, and who they aren't?" Laith asked.

"Take it easy, Laith," Bolan said. "I don't suppose this incident has inspired you to lend me back my equipment for self-protection," the big man asked the captain.

Blake shook his head. "No luck. If you want an escort, I'll lend you one of my men."

Bolan frowned, then noticed something, or someone, over Blake's shoulder. "Fine. I'll take Staff Sergeant Wesley."

Blake looked back at Wesley, who looked like a deer caught in the headlights. "Is that fine with you, soldier?"

Wesley gave a curt nod. "Sir, yes, sir!"

"Good. You're going with Colonel Stone and his party, then," Blake ordered. "Just remember, I want you back here. Alive and in one piece."

"Sir?" Wesley asked.

"I want you back alive. Even if that means that you have to abandon Colonel Stone. He's proved he can take care of himself."

"Sir!" Wesley answered. The man looked conflicted. He didn't like the idea of letting fellow soldiers on the same side die.

Blake didn't like it, either. But he had a duty to the men in his team. He ate, slept, and drank, sweated and bled with them. Their lives were important to him, more important than any other soldier's. It was unit integrity, a knot of loyalty, duty, command and friendship that couldn't be undone by a few strands. He wouldn't like having Stone, Rosenberg and Khan die on his watch, but he wasn't going to sacrifice even the most junior of his noncoms.

"I'll make sure your man returns to you unharmed," Bolan promised.

Blake tried to hide his surprise, but couldn't.

WESLEY WATCHED skeptically as Rosenberg unlocked her safe-house door and let the men in.

"I'm not loving this idea, Theresa," he told her.

She paused, confusion coloring her features for a moment. "You mean about having two men you don't know hanging around with me?"

"Seems that since we've met this guy, you've come under enemy fire twice. And we only met them a couple hours ago," Wesley said.

"Once an hour, that's not so bad for him," she said. There was an impish grin on her face. Those beautiful green eyes sparkled with wit and allure, making Wesley look away, inwardly wincing as he felt himself being dragged in by her beauty. "Robert?" she said.

"I'm sorry. I'm not looking forward to seeing you get hurt," Wesley answered.

"Who says I'm going to get hurt?" she asked.

"A bunch of really angry goombas we kicked out of power, who are still packing enough rifles to shoot up half the country. That's who," Wesley explained.

She sighed. "I've had people out to get me before. I'll live."

"I'm serious, Theresa."

"Call me Tera," she said.

"Tera...sorry..."

"I'm serious, too, Robert."

Wesley reflexively bared his teeth, then calmed himself. "You say you can trust him, so tell me, is Stone his real name?"

"I can't confirm or deny that for you. It's not my place. I can tell you, though, even though we only worked together once, I trust him with every ounce of my being."

Wesley hung his head. "I see."

Geren touched his chin lightly, lifting his eyes to meet hers. "I understand you're worried about me. And I'm worried about you, too. And I would worry about Stone, but he can take care of himself, and he's taken care of me in the past."

"He charges in wild-assed—"

"He can be as stealthy or as audacious as circumstances warrant," Geren said defensively. "And he won't let me down."

Wesley sighed. There was going to be no winning this fight.

"Robert, I know you don't like it, but I also don't want you involved in our investigation. Stone and I are going after, I think, the same people, and there's going to be a lot of gunplay."

"Then have a soldier at your back, at least."

"Captain Blake wants you back alive. And I don't want to see you hurt," Geren cut him off.

"Sorry. He said come back if possible. That was my priority. I'm also supposed to keep an eye on you and Colonel Stone," Wesley replied. "Don't try to leave me behind."

"I don't see the harm in you tagging along." A powerful, but subtle voice spoke, startling Wesley. He looked up to see Colonel Stone seemingly appear out of nowhere. He was shaken for a moment.

"Thank you, Colonel, sir."

"Don't call me sir," Bolan replied. "I work for a living."

He offered his hand. Some of the distrust and jealousy that Wesley was hanging onto evaporated in the face of the gesture. Finally, the Green Beret took the stranger's hand. "Sorry for being so much trouble."

"You're not any trouble. Just please don't interfere with me getting fresh weapons," Bolan said.

Wesley looked at Geren, then nodded. "I wasn't going to have Tera go into harm's way without someone adequately equipped on her side."

Bolan smiled. "Good. Captain Blake won't have a problem with that?"

Wesley looked around. "Captain who? Problem with what?"

Bolan nodded and gave Wesley a clap on the shoulder.

5

Tera Geren shooed Wesley away to settle in the safehouse before turning to Bolan.

"I'll need a medical kit to take care of things," he said casually.

Geren threw her arms around his shoulders and squeezed tight. "I missed you, big guy!" She felt him tense for a second, then he relaxed slightly. She broke off the hug and smiled at him. "I'm sorry. It's just good to see a friendly face."

"I can tell," Bolan answered her. "And I can sympathize."

He dropped his battle harness to the ground, the forty pounds of kit banging on the wooden floor like a bag of hammers. Geren crooked an eyebrow at the payload, then noticed he was peeling out of his blacksuit's top.

"Where's the rest of your stuff?" she asked. "We can probably swing by and pick it up sometime tomorrow." She glanced out the window, and saw the graying of the dawn. "Make that today."

"And how do you know I have more stuff?" Bolan asked.

"You gave up your guns too easily," she responded. "Plus, I know you're prone to having more than just the shirt on your back."

"We had spare ammo and grenades in a car not far from

where we met up," Bolan admitted. "Trouble is, I didn't bring spare firearms. I had planned to replenish my stocks from what we got from the enemy."

When she turned, she saw him stripped down to the waist, fresh bruises and the gunshot wound on his arm standing out against the tracks of toned muscle, bronzed skin and crisscross of scar tissue that made up his torso. The crosshatch of whitened, smooth lines of healed skin were a road map of a life lived in danger. The bloody smear dripping along one biceps came from a slash that would be yet another streak.

"I've got some painkillers for the stitching."

"I'd prefer to do without," Bolan said.

"Not even local anesthetic?" she asked.

"Do you have that?"

She rooted through the kitbox for a moment. "Not really."

"Then why offer what you don't have?" Bolan asked.

Geren took a deep breath and rolled her eyes. "I'm trying to make you feel more comfortable. You've got a gunshot wound, and you're just sitting there, all expressionless, and expect me to dig a needle into your skin and sew your arm shut."

Bolan shrugged, then winced at the movement of his injured arm. "I deal with the pain."

"It doesn't hurt?"

"I'm not that numb. I just don't let it get to me. If I'm taking painkillers, I can't tell when I'm pushing my injuries too hard. I also don't like having my head all cloudy," Bolan told her.

Geren shrugged and began closing the slash. With the last suture pulled shut, six in all, she wrapped his arm in paper tape to keep the stitches from shifting under the skin. Bolan moved his arm, checking his range of motion, and seemed satisfied with it.

THEIR PRIORITIES WERE being taken in order. After rest and recuperation, Bolan and his allies were sufficiently recovered from their hectic night at the start of afternoon. Medical care and some sleep had the Executioner feeling at least back in battle condition.

Bolan filled his empty stomach with a half loaf of bread and some dried beef jerky. A handful of multivitamins would handle the rest of his nutritional needs. It wasn't perfect, but Bolan did what he could with what he had. Food was fuel, and no matter what he laid his hands on, when he had the opportunity, he topped himself off.

"Next order of business," he said to the assembled crew, "we're going to need some guns."

"I think that's directed toward me," Geren spoke up.

Bolan gave her a friendly nod. "Blake didn't disarm you. That means he eventually got tired of trying to."

"Golly, Batman. That's scary when you show that kind of deduction," Geren quipped.

Bolan just shook his head. "I'd prefer you gear up from Tera's stash too, Wesley," he said.

"I'm not going to risk leaving behind clues that Green Berets are on a search-and-destroy mission, not when I'm supposed to be keeping out of the fighting," Wesley answered. "I'll gladly trade in for someone else's gear."

"Good," Bolan said. "Laith, do you have any problem with working with the Mossad?"

Laith gave Geren a glance, his face screwed in an indecipherable expression. Geren squirmed uncomfortably.

"You don't have a problem working together," Bolan said.

"The Khans have been the Mossad local contacts for operations against the Taliban and al Qaeda in Afghanistan for a long time, Colonel," Laith admitted finally. "My family isn't too interested in a bunch of foreigners thinking they can murder, rape and otherwise bully people in our homeland."

"They give us intel, safehouses and storage points for us to make excursions into Pakistan," Geren told Bolan. "The Kashmir might be a reason for a nuclear war between Pakistan and India, but those nukes could also quite easily be used in support of a terrorist operation against Israel."

"I won't tell," Bolan said. He looked to Wesley who was staring off into space.

The young captain jerked back to attention as he realized the others were looking at him. "What?"

"I don't think he heard anything that would result in his brakes failing on a mountain road in his future," Geren quipped. "I'm not naive enough to think that we haven't been watched. It's just that the Pakistanis shouldn't ever find out about anything."

"I'm not telling Pakistan jack shit about anything but how to sit and spin," Wesley answered.

"Good. We'll gear up and start hunting again come sunset," Bolan explained. "Any good leads?"

"Well, I'm pretty sure they'd have ditched the car by now, but there was a gold Peugeot that got shot up during the ambush back at HQ," Wesley said. "The driver seemed to be paying close attention to you three. Most likely you, Tera."

"We saw him peel out and take off," Laith said. "He didn't seem too friendly with the Taliban guys."

"He was an Arab. But who and why?" Bolan asked.

Geren cast her eyes to the floor, avoiding contact with anyone.

"You think he's Palestinian?" Bolan probed.

She stayed motionless. Not even a flinch. But even the absence of a reaction is a reaction. She'd steeled herself against a direct question.

"Tera, you never explained your mission," Bolan said.

"She told us she was investigating the murder of an Israeli national who was in the relief group that got hit," Wesley answered.

"It's a good story, but they wouldn't have sent her. They'd have sent a small army, and they'd be tearing up the countryside with relative impunity," Bolan explained.

"What are you implying, Striker?" Geren asked.

"You work by yourself. You're pretty much a sheet in the wind. Sure, you're a full-fledged agent, but you get thrown into situations where Tel Aviv wouldn't want someone scrutinizing its actions. You'd either have to be a crusader with an agenda or a pariah to be stuck on solo missions. You're one or the other to get the jobs you get."

"Which one are you," Geren countered. She tried to look upset, but her anger was as much reflecting inward as toward the Executioner.

Bolan smiled at Geren. The fireball wasn't going to wither with just a gentle breeze. "I'm a man doing my duty," he said.

"A little of both, then," she answered.

"And your job?"

"Not going to ask me why they think they can leave me running around on my own? Why they think I'm expendable?" Geren said angrily.

Bolan shook his head. "It's not our concern now. The Mossad is worried about the killings of a UN relief worker, but I don't think they're as interested in the murder of one of their nationals as to who caused the murder."

Her eyes flashed with emerald anger again. Bolan had her,

and he frowned. He was not enjoying peeling away her cover story, leaving her exposed and vulnerable. She stared at him, the anger melting away as she noticed his own growing guilt.

"Tera, we need to know what we're up against, and you keeping your mouth shut—" Bolan said.

"They call themselves Abraham's Dagger," Geren admitted. "At least that's what they claimed once we found out who they were."

"What did they call themselves before they got exposed?" Wesley asked.

"Mossad agents and Israeli soldiers," she grumbled. "It was an organization that was on both sides of government sanction in the administration. Private citizens and officers, troops and politicians, from all walks of life, all pushing the government toward harsher and harsher measures against the 'Palestinian problem.'"

"And you got caught in the middle of this?" Sympathy filled Laith's voice.

Geren shrugged. "It's a job. Just a job. Most of the people I work with don't like the fact that collateral damage happens when we go up against scumbags like Hamas or hard-core Palestinian thugs. Using an F-16 to blow up an apartment building and a bunch of sleeping children just to get one guy isn't the way we pride ourselves on taking care of business. We're pros, we get the job done, we take care of the guilty and we leave the innocent unhurt."

"Abraham's Dagger would rather go the easy route," Bolan said.

"You know vigilantes," she answered.

Bolan felt that shot as sure as if she intended it for his gut. The Executioner had long walked the line between being a man on a mission and being a cold-blooded murderer. He chose his battles, doing so when he felt the law wouldn't take a hand, or was powerless to act.

Bolan limited himself in his war plans, however. He would never accept civilian losses. He risked his life to save people from the spillover of his conflicts against Animal Man. When he struck, he was always dead certain of his prey's guilt. Most of the time, if there was any doubt, he tried to cut and run, preferring to continue the battle on his own terms later on. There had been a few exceptions, and those few instances left scars seared across his soul far worse than the streaks of whitened flesh on his skin.

It would have been easier, even safer, to wage his war like the tactics of Abraham's Dagger Tera was describing.

But he would never give in to that type of battle.

Jaw locked, Bolan nodded. "I know vigilantes."

"They've gone too far. For the longest time, they almost stepped across the line. People were willing to ignore them when they made their own punitive strikes against terrorists and their families. The dead child of a terrorist was at least someone who wouldn't grow up to be a terrorist," the Israeli woman said.

Wesley shook his head. "Fucked up way to fight a war."

"Then the Dagger came down on a refugee camp. Maybe it was soldiers on active duty, maybe it wasn't. They went through and slaughtered a hundred men, women and children, and wounded almost a thousand more. A few UN workers spotted them, but they were transferred out as fast as possible," Geren said. "The UN denied that their people saw anything, but Abraham's Dagger didn't buy it. People started dying. Two automobile accidents. One poor guy drowned in his bathtub after someone piled three cinder blocks on his chest."

"And now they come to Afghanistan?" Laith asked.

"Sofia DeLarroque was a witness to the massacre that happened in a refugee camp called Shafeeq. When she came over here, it was an effort to make her unreachable," Geren explained. "Trouble is, Mossad knows, Abraham's Dagger knows. So guess which redheaded stepchild gets sent to take these guys on?"

"Witnesses reported there were Afghan soldiers," Wesley said. "Former Taliban enforcers, sorry."

Laith nodded. "Verbal shorthand. Those dogs aren't worthy to be described by my country's name, but then, my country was slothlike in throwing off their yoke. Enough of that. The ex-Taliban types can be explained easily. They're hard up for money. They came here hired by rich and fanatical Saudi and Yemeni citizens. Sons of princes and oil magnates, looking to make the perfect Islamic state. Now, with the bosses dead or in hiding, they're hiring themselves out to whoever wants to give them some cash. So we have fanatics who got bit by the pragmatism bug," Laith said. "No great causes they can die for, so they might as well get paid to kill for something."

"Terrorists have been that way across history," Bolan spoke up. "They start with a devotion to a cause, but if they don't die off or end up in jail, they learn there's a profit to be made. There might be old believers still out there, still true blue to their ideology, but they're either in organizations too poor to engage in real operations, or they're fangless in what actions they do take."

"This is all well and good, but we started talking about a car watching you, Tera," Wesley interrupted.

"If he was watching me and took off when things got nasty, then that means we have Palestinians on the scene too," she stated. "And while we really can't call them friends, they aren't going to be interested in attacking me because I'm doing the footwork in locating the people they really want to hit."

"Abraham's Dagger," Bolan said. "It's going to be a cross fire. The Dagger's going to be hunting the UN workers currently in country. And we have Palestinians racing with us to hunt down the Dagger members. Throw in the United States Special Forces watching to see that everyone behaves, and we'll be having a four-way dance."

"Well, I can help smooth things over with Blake, if possible," Wesley offered. "And maybe we can form a temporary truce with the Palestinians. Maybe."

Bolan nodded. "I'd prefer that. Trouble is, if we come to their doorstep, there's no guarantee that they won't try kicking us off."

"And they'd do the kicking to the tune of an AK," Geren muttered.

"Bingo," Bolan said. "So we're going to have to make a decision on how we're going to deal with them."

The woman shrugged. "I'm all for extra muscle on our side for once. If we go hunting for the Palestinian team, we'll probably force a shootout. In the field, we might be able to form a truce."

"The enemy of my enemy," Laith said.

"I just want you to make sure you're all certain who your targets are. We can avoid an extra force gunning for us if we act smart," Bolan stated. "If not, stay close to cover and keep in communication with the rest of us. We'll pull you out. Am I clear?"

The other three nodded in unison. "Crystal clear."

Bolan didn't feel a wave of sweeping inspiration from his "army," but at least they seemed to have their heads all together. They had a common goal, and at least gave lip service to working together. "Now let's get some guns," he said.

THE STASH WAS HIDDEN in the remains of an old Soviet-occupation-era garage. While the shell of the building had been chewed away by battle and erosion, the inside was in good enough condition that the stairwell to the basement was undamaged. The center of the basement was taken up by the smashed remains of a hydraulic lift. The only sign that the garage was anything but ruins was a door that was solid. It was weathered, but the locks were stainless steel, the hinges were new and shielded behind more steel, and the whole thing was painted slapdash with splotches of black and brown to simulate rust and fire damage. Inside, hidden behind empty cardboard boxes, were crates of equipment.

Crates that had already been opened.

"Abraham's Dagger was here," Bolan said.

"They would know the best spots to go shopping. There are other arsenals we can use," Geren replied.

"We'd be wasting time running across Afghanistan," Bolan answered. "We'll take what we need here."

She nodded. "Okay."

Bolan looked over the choices he had. He was pleased to note that there were radios with earphones and throat mikes. That would make a lot of difference in a combat situation. Communication was vital, and when he worked with others, he was always glad to have the best possible electronics on hand. He took eight, four spares in case the radios got damaged.

The Executioner was pleased to come across a cache of .44 Magnum Desert Eagles. Though the guns were Israeli designed, the stockpile of Magnum autoloaders were actually the Minnesota-built Magnum Research designs. Bolan loaded a pair into his war bag along with six 50-round boxes of 240-grain hollowpoint bullets.

"Check out the micro-Uzis," Geren said.

"You don't have any stores of Uzi magazines here," Bolan protested.

"These are the Mark 2s. They take regular and extended Glock pistol magazines. The most popular 9 mm pistol in the world," she explained.

Bolan picked up the Uzi pistol. He flipped back the folding stock, then folded it forward, checking to see how it handled single-handedly. "Good. We'll take eight, and all the Glock mags and 9 mm ammo we can carry."

"The home office isn't going to appreciate all their inventory walking off in someone else's war bags," Geren said as she watched Bolan feed a magazine into the butt of the Uzi.

"Then the home office should keep its so-called patriots from slaughtering refugees and relief workers," Bolan answered. He found a box of shoulder harnesses for the Uzi pistols. "Sorry, Tera."

"You don't have to get on my case," she answered. Rage flashed in her emerald eyes before she managed to pull it together as well. "I'm chasing those bastards, same as you are. They stepped over a line we didn't want them to, either."

"So how come they're still on the loose?"

"Eight of them are in jail. Another three are dead, resisting arrest," Geren replied. "But they were handled on Israeli soil, and they were handled quietly."

"Sorry. I didn't know."

"That was the point of handling it on our soil. That's the point of sending me, by myself, to take these animals down on my own. We don't want it advertised that our people are overreacting and are behind murdering children for the sake of bloodthirsty revenge."

Bolan nodded. "I'm not going to leak anything. Like you

hinted before, I'm as much a loose cannon, a cat that walks by himself as you are. I do my duty and that's protecting the innocent and punishing the guilty."

Geren's face softened, and Bolan could see an apology already forming. He shook his head and put a finger to his lips.

"Let's chalk the tension up to incomplete intel," he said. "I don't allow myself to get upset, usually."

"That warrior monk bullshit only goes so far. You are just a man, remember?" Geren said. "Unless you really are bulletproof."

"Nope," Bolan answered. "I've just been smart enough to avoid bad luck, and lucky enough when I was caught flat-footed, and quick enough to handle things before I even had to recognize I was in trouble."

"So it's not all in the reflexes," Geren stated.

Bolan turned away and tried on the Uzi harness, pistol locked in place, stock folded.

"What are you trying to dance away from?" the Israeli agent asked.

Bolan looked up, then sighed. "I just don't think that going into the metaphysics of my survival is important. I'd rather concentrate on what I have to do, and how to do it well."

"Just keep putting one boot in front of the other and don't think about how far the walk is," Geren said.

"One way to put it," Bolan answered. "I'm glad I have someone I know and is a proved quantity on my side. It makes things easier."

"Even if you do worry about me?" Geren asked, smiling.

Bolan looked down at her, shook his head and stepped away, slipping a jacket over the Uzi harness. "We've got work to do, Tera."

He didn't allow himself a glance back at her.

6

"Damnation," Rhodin growled, giving the tent post a kick.

"Relax," Steiner said in his soft, Zen master voice. He was sitting still, and as Rhodin paced, he seemed to be the center of a drain of nervous energy. With each pass, it was harder and harder for the Abraham's Dagger commando to keep up his frustration.

"How do you do that?" Rhodin asked.

Steiner looked up and managed a smile that didn't reach his sad eyes. Nothing ever reached those haunted orbs. "Clean living I guess."

Rhodin wrinkled his nose. "We got one target, but you didn't give us much of a chance to interrogate her about the others, did you?"

"She was halfway out the window and ready to bolt," Steiner answered as if Rhodin had asked him why he'd put too much sugar in their coffee. "I had to stop her."

"So you killed her," Rhodin answered.

Steiner shrugged. "We have Soze and the others tracking the other women down."

Rhodin shook his head.

The tent opened and Rhodin spun, half expecting to see one of their Taliban allies poking his head through. Instead, it was Soze himself.

"Speak of the devil, and he shall come," Steiner said, almost singsong.

Soze's swarthy, tanned face twisted into a sneer at the calm assassin, then he turned back to Rhodin. "We tried to take care of the Geren woman."

"She's still alive," Rhodin stated. He gave the tent's centerpost another kick of frustration. "Bad enough the Mossad is turning us into criminals for doing what they're too puny to do, now they're sending a woman after us!"

"Not a woman. Geren," Steiner whispered.

Rhodin snarled and paced to one corner of the tent, grabbing a cigarette. "Bad enough it's a woman, but the granddaughter of a fucking Nazi."

"Who better to hunt Jews than a Nazi?" Soze asked. "Naughty Jews chased after by a squeaky clean little goose-stepping dyke."

"I wouldn't underestimate her," Steiner said. He stood up, and the swirling vortex of calm disappeared. "What happened?"

"We had our friends watching the American base camp, watching for her return. When she arrived, she had two newcomers with her," Soze answered. "Our Taliban rejects described them as one local and one American."

Steiner turned his thick, boltlike head toward Soze.

"One recognized the local as one of the Khan brothers," Soze said.

"The other. Tall American? Black hair?"

"Yes," Soze said.

Steiner's jaw set.

"What's wrong?" Rhodin asked. Steiner's normally impassive face suddenly went as hard as stone, even the eyes narrowed, as if focusing his incredible mental power into a laser beam.

"Let me guess. They opened up on the American stranger,

and he was instrumental in breaking the ambush. You suffered nearly complete losses too," Steiner said.

Soze's jaw dropped. "How—"

"I know the pattern."

"The good news is, one of our men kept under cover. He didn't join in the fight and watched as the three of them, and an American Green Beret, were sent off. The American didn't have a weapon anymore," Soze concluded.

Steiner shook his head and glanced across to Rhodin. "We should put a team on the weapons cache."

Rhodin looked at him. "Why?"

"A good soldier never passes up a chance to rearm, and Geren knows about the cache. He'll be looking for quality gear, and that's what we have. Chances are, they'll also be looking for any clues we left behind."

Rhodin snorted. "We didn't leave any traces behind."

"Everyone leaves clues behind," Steiner replied. "Just by the fact that we took stuff from a Mossad forward cache—"

Rhodin slapped his forehead and took another step toward kicking the tent post when Steiner raised one big, callused hand and pressed it to his chest.

"Please don't do that again," Steiner growled.

"Why?" Rhodin asked.

"I don't want the tent falling on me," Steiner answered. "I'll lead the team against Geren and the American."

"I can't risk that," Rhodin said.

"You can't risk Geren's new ally′ causing us trouble," Steiner grumbled. "Surely you've heard the stories."

"Rumors! Fantasies!" Rhodin snapped back.

"About who?" Soze asked.

"Some people call him Al-Askari," Steiner answered.

"Others just call him the Soldier. He's responsible for destroying countless terrorist groups."

"So then he'd be on our side?" Soze asked.

"We're operating as a terrorist group," Rhodin retorted. "There's not a shred of proof that he exists."

"Except dead terrorists from pole to pole," Steiner countered. "Terrorists who ended up dead for no other reason than their actions brought down the vengeance of the Soldier."

"Oh no…" Soze's voice trailed off.

"You believe this crap too?" Rhodin asked.

Steiner frowned. "Better safe than sorry. We'll stage an ambush at the cache."

"Even if it isn't this supersoldier, he's still someone who's going to be another threat at our backs, sir," Soze spoke up.

Rhodin couldn't argue with that logic. "All right. Saddle up and give them a warm welcome."

Steiner nodded. "A very warm welcome."

LIKE A SNAKE COILED in the shadows to avoid being addled by the sunlight, Greb Steiner nestled behind the scope of his Zastava M76, an 8 mm Mauser round under the hammer, ready to spit across the four hundred yards between him and the cache.

Rhodin wanted him on hand for the hit against Tera Geren and her mysterious allies, but he didn't want the sad-eyed assassin anywhere near the action. Beside him, manning an RPK machine gun, was Soze. Both were relegated to watching and coordinating the action from afar, keeping under cover and out of sight. Throat microphones and earpieces conveyed messages between the Israelis and their Taliban dupes.

Steiner had less respect for the men closing in on the four people at the cache than he held for the bacteria that helped him digest food in his lower intestine. The militiamen hadn't questioned why six strangers came to their lands and spoke perfect Arabic, even if it was in an Egyptian dialect. They merely accepted the money, the guns, the support and leadership of trained warriors to continue their jihad against the invading Westerners who sought to wipe away the decades of a perfect Islamic paradise.

Their idealism had been flushed away in the hard rain of American rage post-9/11, their government destroyed, their organization disrupted by a cleansing storm. Now, they were living, bullying who they could in order to have money and food and a roof over their heads. They were no longer gods sitting upon a backward people, vampires who sucked the blood of a people too tired from a Soviet invasion and too frightened of an organized, fanatical intrusion. They were ticks, fleas. Parasites who burrowed into the skin and scurried away from scratching fingers, drinking dollops of vital life from people here and there, leaving behind the disease of fear and distrust.

But they made good cannon fodder.

Steiner and his team were fluent in Arab dialects, and chose Egyptian as that was who they had tanned themselves to most resemble. Back when they still bore the stink of legitimacy in the Israeli government, they were undercover agents, trained to sound and look like native Palestinians, Syrians, Lebanese, anyone who could be an enemy. The Taliban thought the weapons cache was an Egyptian holdout. A safeguard against possible trouble from nearby Iran or Pakistan.

A safe enough lie that was close to the truth. Only the national ownership was off, and that was only by one geographic step to the left.

The ex-militiamen didn't care. Cash was coming to them. Their hands were wrapped around guns. They instilled terror.

And riding along in their shadow, silent and invisible, were the warriors of Abraham's Dagger, cutting away any who would betray the true identities of those who brought justice to the murdered children of Israel by murdering the children of their enemies. Steiner felt a cold calm, as always. Avoiding the cooking sun in the shadows, his heart was still and easy, hands steady as stone, eyes locked like lasers on his enemies as they left two outside to guard them and give warning.

Steiner was not afraid of getting in close, of going nose to nose in combat with his enemies, no matter how strong, how armored, how tough they were, but his orders were clear.

Observe only.

The sniper rifle was only a precaution—in case they came under fire from below. Or if the enemy managed to capture one of their Taliban cohorts alive.

An 8 mm round between the shoulder blades would slice off any attempts at interrogation.

Steiner figured the logic.

If he and Soze got into close combat and failed, even their corpses would provide volumes of information to a determined and skilled specialist. Diet. Dust. Residue. They'd be flaming arrows pointing back across the countryside to Rhodin and the others.

Steiner was willing to die to fight off the barbarian hordes laying siege to his nation, but he wasn't so stupid as to die and leave himself as decomposing evidence to betray his brothers.

No. If this ambush failed, there were other ways to insure that Geren and her friends would end up going to their just reward. Throwing themselves after a failed assault would be pointless.

Soze mopped his brow, fist clenched around the pistol grip of the RPK. "We should just hose down those two and let our pals drop grenades down the stairwell."

"That might work," Steiner answered. He settled the cross-hairs of his rifle on the face of a tall, young American with a goatee, standing near a smaller, native looking man. Both were dressed in jumpsuits and battle vests. The American looked in his midtwenties, and he most definitely wasn't the stranger who set off the alarm bells in his head the night before. If anything, he recognized the youngster as one of the so-called faceless soldiers who had been assigned to the town. He imagined the young man's face exploding as 195 grains of supersonic lead punched through bone and brain matter, smashing it apart like a rotted melon.

However, Steiner kept his finger off the trigger.

He wanted all four out in the open, burdened with packages, flat-footed and off guard.

"Tighten up on that right flank," he ordered.

The militiamen were not soldiers. They weren't used to dealing with enemies unless they outgunned and outnumbered them. Against the concentrated force of the American military, they evaporated like gasoline spilled on a street. From hiding and ambush, using the tactics of craven cowards, they were hot shit using car bombs and bullets sprayed wildly out the doors of speeding automobiles.

Their kind was almost enough to break the resolution of the servicemen standing watch against the barbarians.

Almost.

There was movement now, from the stairwell. Tera Geren was up, and she had two duffel bags, her hands and exposed forearms corded with the strain of holding their weight. The young American ran to her side, trying to take one of the bags, talking softly with her. She spoke harshly, nodding toward his slung rifle.

The man paused, then stepped away from the burdened Tera Geren, both hands on his rifle, eyes sweeping around.

A small, canlike object sailed out of the stairwell, trailing a tail of smoke like a spool of gray cotton.

As if on cue, as the smoke grenade bounced off the ground, the three people suddenly dropped to the ground.

A heartbeat later, the rattle of automatic rifles filled the air.

That's when the tall stranger emerged from the basement, a weapon in each fist, muzzle-flashes flickering like lightning from the hands of a wrathful god.

MACK BOLAN WAS LAST OUT of the cache, weighed down with three war bags, his muscles coiled like steel serpents around his arms against the weight of his gear.

There was a curt whistling noise, and Bolan stopped halfway up the steps. Geren and Wesley were discussing the Green Beret's task. He was their guard, and he had to keep his eyes sharp and weapons tight in hand, ready for pitched battle.

The whistle, however, was a low trilling sound, like wind slicing through the mountain passes. The Executioner's spine tingled as the note cut off, replaced by Laith's voice.

"Come on guys," he said. Bolan couldn't see him, but the sound of Laith's voice traveled from off to one side to closer to the others. "Let's quit bitching. I'm dying for a smoke here."

Bolan set his bags down and reached for a canister grenade. The young Afghan lion was trying to say something, but not be blatantly obvious so that anyone watching, within ambush range, could hear them.

Wesley chuckled. "What brand you smoke? Camels?"

"Not funny," Laith answered. "In fact, I'm deadly serious."

There was no mistaking it now. Laith was asking Geren and Wesley to get moving, asking for smoke cover and saying the situation was deadly serious…but not asking what was keeping Bolan so long.

The Executioner popped the pin on the smoker and tossed it sailing over his allies. Bodies struck the ground and gunfire ripped the air. Bolan plunged his hands into one war bag, hauling out an item that he slung over his neck on its nylon strap.

The Executioner had sprung the trap early. He filled his fists with the Desert Eagle and the Uzi and stormed up the steps. He spotted a trio of Taliban militiamen fanning the smoke with rifle fire from the cover of a shattered storefront, and swung both guns toward them. Parabellum and .44 Magnum slugs flew in a swarm of deadly leaden hornets at his targets, bodies jerking and spinning, tumbling lifelessly to hard, heartless concrete. Blood poured from crater-sized impact wounds on one of the gunmen, while another who had taken a burst of fire from the Uzi was still twitching, trying to reach his fallen weapon. A mercy burst finished him.

"Laith! Wesley! Get the gear! Tera, make for the Rover!" Bolan ordered. He was seeking fresh targets.

Wesley and Laith retreated, their rifles raking a Toyota pickup that served as cover for a fire team. Their movement and fire drew enemy reaction, muzzle-flashes grabbing the Executioner's attention as he swung the twin Israeli pistols against his foes. More thunder crackled and burst from his hands, one by one enemy weapons going silent under his onslaught before the Desert Eagle and Uzi each ran dry.

There was a pause as, even through the smoke, Bolan saw surprised faces registering the sudden silence coming from the tall wraith in combat black. They saw him lower his handguns to his side, dropping them softly to the ground. Bolan's ice-cold eyes glared back at them, keeping them enthralled at the suddenly disarmed angel of death, dropping his tools.

That's when one noticed the M-4 slung around his neck, spare magazines clipped to the central magazine tripling the firepower of the rifle. He started to yell, but the Executioner's hand was on the pistol grip, pivoting the carbine on its sling and pulling the trigger. A sweep of 5.56 mm slugs shredded its brutal path. Four close-packed Taliban militiamen were torn open at the rib cage by transsonic slugs plowing through flesh and pulversizing against bone.

Bodies tumbled in soggy heaps. Wild, frantic gunfire now ignored Laith and Wesley as they hastily scrambled to drag the supplies to the Land Rover. Tera Geren turned over the engine, its roar lost to all but the Executioner in the fusillade of response to him. The Taliban veterans were showing their true colors, emptying their rifles without any effort to control the violent, bucking recoil of their weapons. All they achieved was to pepper empty air and loose chunks of broken wall that Bolan weaved around.

The Executioner tapped off 2- and 3-shot bursts, taking the time to make dead certain there was a body behind the front sight post of the M-4. Every pull of the trigger, ejected only a couple of shots, and ended with an enemy gunman screaming, pieces of his head or torso evaporating.

Amateur predators fell like deer in the headlights before a trained, veteran hunter.

Even so, a lucky shot, deflected off a hunk of stone, struck Bolan, glancing off his shoulder. He winced at the hammer force of the blow, his mind instantly registering that it struck where the armored, load-bearing vest covered his torso. The shoulder strap kept the bullet from penetrating, but it hurt like hell. The Executioner took that as a hint to duck behind a foot-thick slab of wall and snap the magazine around to a fresh one.

Once reloaded, Bolan swung around the side, spotting the Land Rover on the roll. He plucked a grenade from his pocket, spotting a group of riflemen racing around the column of choking smoke. They probably sought to come up on the vehicle's blind side, but popping the pin, Bolan whipped the grenade, hardball style at the group.

The egg-shaped minibomb struck the chest of the lead gunman hard enough to make him stumble, rifle clattering from shocked fingers. It was only in the next heartbeat that the militiaman realized what had struck him and he tried backing away from it. It was too late. His comrades slammed into him from behind, trying to continue their rush toward their enemies' vehicle. Bolan shouldered his rifle, seeking more targets as the grenade's fuse burned to zero and detonated.

The Executioner was bringing hell to the ambush party, ripping off more short bursts of precision fire toward a pair of gunmen had hunkered down, trying to pin in the Land Rover. However, this time, the enemy was wedged in too tight behind hard cover. They turned and opened fire on Bolan. They kept themselves low and out of the way. Hailstorms of COMBLOC lead chopped away the stones that he was using for protection. With the bad guys suddenly developing a clue, it was time to bug out, but Bolan was too pinned down, and he'd used his last fragger already.

Wesley and Laith suddenly poked out of the window of the Land Rover, swinging their rifles at the two men firing on Bolan. It took more than a short precision burst apiece. Each of Bolan's allies burned an entire magazine to take out the pair of holed up killers. Geren turned the Rover, rear wheels producing rooster tails of dirt as she fishtailed to a violent halt.

"Get in, Colonel! We're steppin' out!" she roared.

Bolan threw his rifle to Geren and ran low, scooping up the Uzi and the Desert Eagle on the run. With a dive, he was in the back seat next to Laith.

The Rover lurched, and with the odd plunk of a bullet

striking the hardened skin of the big offroad vehicle, they were charging away from the battle scene.

But Bolan knew the worrisome truth.

The enemy knew that they were on the case and had set up an ambush. It had taken alertness, luck, shooting skill and bald audacity to break the back of the ambush. And once more, Bolan had proved his willingness to take a bullet for an ally.

But not before putting a few dozen into his enemies first.

The Land Rover charged over the broken road, escaping to let its occupants fight another day.

7

The knock at Mikela Bronson's door made her heart leap, and her hand slid into the desk drawer for the little pistol she kept there. It wasn't much, but at least she wouldn't go down without a fight, unlike Sofia.

The knock repeated itself, and Mikela stepped from behind her desk. "Come in."

Her office was small, but she had a filing cabinet that she could use for cover if the newcomers were hostile. She didn't know what to think, especially with someone coming to visit her at midnight while she was on duty.

She didn't think that the terrorists would be polite enough to knock before entering the office of someone they were coming to kill, but maybe they were making sure someone was there to shoot in the first place. She tensed as the door opened.

"Don't be alarmed Dr. Bronson," said a warm, gentle voice. It was deep and strong, yet held no hostility. It reminded her of her favorite instructor back at Johns Hopkins, the voice of a man who could break bad news to you and yet comfort you in the same sentence.

What stepped in, however, was no kindly man in a white lab coat.

He was a tall black-clad commando, face smeared with

grime, bedecked in what looked like the latest U.S. Cavalry catalog gear. She was taken aback by his appearance, but he smiled at her.

"Forgive my appearance, Doctor," he said. "My name is Colonel Brandon Stone, and I'm here to ask if you'd please accompany me into protective custody for a few days."

Mikela was speechless, and she looked down at the pop-gun in her hand. "I can fend for myself," she said.

"Not with that," the man told her.

"I'm a pretty good shot." Mikela swallowed hard, then noticed there were others out in the hall. All of them were dressed for a fight. "You don't look like you're going to stay away from any danger," she said.

"We're not. But we're going to keep you out of the sights of the bad guys," the only woman in the group told her. Mikela was surprised that such a small-statured woman could carry the full pockets on her vest and the huge rifle in her delicate little hands.

As if reading the doubt on her face, the big man spoke again. "Dr. Bronson—Mikela—there are some very danger-ous men after you. They're not merely ex-Taliban militiamen. There are six former members of a covert Israeli black-ops unit who have stepped over the line. The Mossad and the U.S. Justice Department are working together to bring them to jus-tice, but we have to make sure you're in safe hands first."

He held up a vest. "It's ballistic nylon with trauma plates. It weighs a ton, and I don't promise it will become comfort-able any time soon, but it's better than a sucking chest wound."

Mikela reached out and took the vest, almost dropping it. The weight of the Kevlar pulled her arm down, and she stum-bled forward.

That's when the window shattered. A hand flashed out and grabbed her upper arm, yanking her toward the door while a massive shape lunged past her. The compression waves of bullets leaving the barrel of a powerful weapon hammered in the tight quarters of the office, the sound of each gunshot penetrating deep in her gut. Another pair of hands grabbed her and pulled her and through the doorway, carrying her like a rag doll.

"Go, Rob! Go!" the redheaded woman called out.

Fear cut like a knife through the doctor's stomach, but she remembered what Colonel Stone had said and squirmed into the battle vest. It was tight and weighed heavily on her shoulders.

But it was more comfortable than a sucking chest wound.

LUCK HAD BEEN on the Executioner's side. Had Dr. Mikela Bronson not been thrown off balance by the weight of the protective body armor he'd handed her, she'd have ended up dead, a bullet caving in her rib cage. As it was, they weren't out of danger simply because Wesley was taking her away from the sniper's arc of fire.

Instead, Bolan shouldered his M-4, using the barrel to smash away the remaining glass in the window frame. The scope atop his rifle brought the far side of the street and its rooftops into sharp relief despite the starlit night. It had only taken a moment for Bolan to line up the point of impact and the hole in the window to give him a bearing on where the shooter was. Hammering out half a magazine, he peppered a window on the top floor of the building across the road. There was no glass to shatter, and 5.56 mm rounds kicked out clouds of concrete dust and stone chips in a savage display of his rifle's power.

It wasn't the most outstanding display of ammunition conservation, but it was suppressive fire, and it was only half of one magazine. Bolan held his fire and took cover, waving down Geren. The Israeli ducked behind the desk.

With the cessation of hostilities from the Executioner, there was movement. Bolan made a decision to test his opponent. He presented only the barest fraction of himself. The rifle he carried protected what bit of his face poked around the window frame to look across the street. He kept his arm low, the wall and the weapon likewise protecting his hand and forearm.

The enemy sniper didn't expose himself, but a muzzle-flash exploded across the street, a powerful blast that was accompanied by Bolan flying back into the filing cabinet as what felt like a freight train smashed into his chest. Thrown to the floor, he dropped low, taking a deep breath to replace the one that was squeezed out of him by the god-fist that had hit him. No sparks of agony flared to inform him of a fresh new batch of broken ribs from this close call with death. He felt where the bullet struck and saw a crushed magazine in his pocket, the aluminum caved in as if it were a soda pop can. He pulled the magazine from its place. Bullets spilled across the floor.

Damaged shells spilled gunpowder, and Bolan swept them toward the wall, in case he had to run. He looked at the slug imbedded in the magazine's wall.

"What the hell? Are you okay?" Geren asked.

"I'll live. Keep your head down, though," Bolan told her. He touched his throat mike. "Wesley, you have the doctor?"

"Yeah," the young sergeant's voice came back over the earplug.

"She in her armor yet?" Bolan asked.

"She's dressed not to be killed," Wesley answered.

"That vest won't stop a head shot, and it might not even stop whatever the sniper's using. He's got an 8 mm Mauser," Bolan explained.

Geren lifted her hand. "Is that bad, teacher?"

"It's more powerful than most of the rounds these vests are designed to protect against," Bolan told her. "Not by much, but it is pretty powerful."

Bolan shifted position. "Laith, any movement outside?"

"I've got a couple of bad guys heading for the front door. Want me to—"

"No," Bolan cut off the young Afghan. "I don't want to tip your presence just yet. Hang tight until the bad guys throw more reinforcements at us, or we come to pick you up."

"Ace in the sleeve, over and out!" Laith answered, no disappointment in his words.

Bolan was relieved at that much. He wasn't thrilled to hear about the pair of shooters who were coming through the front of the hospital. At this time of night, most of the patients were in their rooms, but there was still staff about. The last time Abraham's Dagger had sent a Taliban squad into a hospital, it was a scorched-earth policy, and he wasn't sure that policy would change if there was a sniper at work.

"Wesley, you heard that?" Bolan asked.

"Did indeed, Colonel. What should we do?"

"Take Dr. Bronson and slip out the back. Don't attract any attention from the bad guys, and tell any on-call staff to get under cover," Bolan told him.

"And you two?" Wesley asked.

Bolan remembered a term his Able Team friend Hermann Schwarz used a lot.

"We've got to take care of a pest problem."

TERA GEREN SLIPPED OUT of the office first. She slung her rifle, realizing that its length would only snag and trip her up in the halls and doorways of the hospital. Instead, she pulled her micro-Uzi machine pistol from its harness and gave Bolan a nod. A 33-round magazine was in place, and she was confident in her ability to cut through any opposition with the 9 mm chatterbox.

"Laith, any more coming in?" Tera asked.

"Just the two I saw coming in the front. I can't vouch for any other entrances, though, so be careful," Laith answered.

Geren chuckled. "Careful is my middle name."

"Really? Mine's Cornelius. But if you tell anyone, I'll have to kill you."

"Cut the chatter," Bolan's voice intruded. "Find some other way to cool your nerves."

Geren nodded, looking back, expecting to see the big soldier, but he had disappeared. She walked swiftly, keeping herself tight to one wall or the other, always sweeping her eyes in an arc, looking for trouble. Her ears strained for any stray sounds betraying the approach of an enemy.

A nurse stepped out of a room and saw the Israeli terrorist hunter. The nurse seemed almost comedic, dark-faced over a white, old-fashioned outfit, like something out of a cartoon. She paused, her round face wide with surprise. Geren raised her finger to her lips and shook her head. "Get into the patient's room and stay there."

The nurse nodded and disappeared into a room. Geren took three long strides and reached an intersection. An elevator was coming up, its indicator showing the car's progress. The redheaded fireball pressed herself against the desk, crouching low, thankful she was short and already a small target.

The doors hissed open and a single man came out. She tensed but kept her finger off the trigger. The man was a clean shaved Arab, but he didn't look like a local. His dress was too western, and he looked, for all the world, Palestinian.

He could have been a member of Abraham's Dagger. The

Dagger was made up of agents chosen specifically for their ability to blend in with Palestinians and Israeli-born Arabs in the West Bank, the Gaza Strip and other similar territories. But something seemed wrong. He had a weapon, its ugly shape creating an equally ugly bulge under his jacket, but he became more worried as he looked around.

He'd taken a sidestep toward her when she made her presence known.

"Keep your hands where I can see them!" she snapped.

The man froze, and she got a good look at his face.

It was Marid Haytham, and he looked like a deer caught in the headlights. He put his hands out. "There's eight members of Abraham's Dagger's goon squad right on my heels, Geren," he said.

"You know me?" the Israeli agent asked.

"It pays to know my enemies, and the enemies of my enemy. I've been watching you for days."

The woman pondered Marid Haytham's reputation. He was known as a straight shooter, and someone who fought only those who could fight back. In a war where his brethren struck at the unarmed and the helpless as a means of showing the Israeli government their willingness to fight, Haytham limited himself to those whose job it was to get in harm's way. It didn't make him a saint by any stretch, if by some chance she should actually start acknowledging saints, but it did give her pause.

"Get under cover, Haytham," Geren said. "And the first time you turn that gun on me—"

"I know," Haytham growled. He was too smart to get any closer to her. The Palestinian turned and went down the hall, taking cover in an alcove.

"Tera?" Bolan's voice came over the radio. "Who were you talking to?"

"An old friend," Geren answered. "He says we've got eight."

"That much I figured. I've got two in my sights now."

A stairwell door slammed.

"And I have a couple of my own," she answered back, crossing from the desk to the corner of the intersection, watching the two men, weapons held low, enter the hall. They looked both ways but were scanning at chest height, which meant that Geren was below their line of sight.

She lined up a laser on the knees of one of the gunmen and milked the trigger of the Uzi pistol. The Taliban mercenary was sent howling to the floor, his knees and shins blasted to bits, his body hitting tile hard. The weapon in his hands skidded out of his reach just as a second weapon opened up in the hall. The other Dagger dupe was hit by two streams of automatic fire, one from Geren, and one from Haytham.

Ripped apart by twin salvos of lead, the second hit man didn't stand a chance as he struck a wall, spilling over a dirty linen hamper left in the hall.

Geren glanced back at Haytham, who kept his weapon trained on the dying gunman, pointed away from her.

She didn't love the situation she was in, but she could live with it.

Elsewhere, thunder echoed through the halls.

BOLAN DIDN'T LIKE the sudden cryptic attitude Tera Geren had developed after her hasty conversation with a newcomer. But that wasn't his immediate worry as the two gunmen he saw were joined by another pair of Taliban locals.

Three of them looked like Taliban.

One didn't.

To a less familiar eye, he would have passed for Palestinian on a good ~~night~~ But the Executioner had faced far too many enemies over the years. One of the things that kept him alive was his sharp senses and his ability to identify people almost instantly.

The fourth man was a member of Abraham's Dagger, and he was in charge of the operation. Bolan took a sidestep, bringing up his Uzi pistol to deal with the team leader. The sudden flash of movement, however, had to have been enough to activate the paranoia-wired reflexes of the Dagger hit man. He lurched suddenly, stepping so that a Taliban gunman was between him and Bolan's line of fire.

Since it wasn't an innocent hostage, Bolan fired anyway, sending four 9 mm slugs peppering into the Arab thug's chest. The man gave a grunt, then steadied himself, swinging up his rifle and crying out in rage and shock. The Executioner didn't waste time concerning himself as to why four Parabellum bullets weren't enough to knock the terrorist off his feet. He simply took a long sidestep, hit a crouch, aimed for the man's face and blew it apart with another salvo of manstoppers.

Even as he died, the bulletproof killer triggered his AK with a heart-stopping display of thunder and lightning. Bolan saw him strike the ground, and saw the telltale blue nylon shell of body armor poking out under his robe rags. That mystery was solved, but the soldier had other things on his mind as he scrambled for the protection of a heavy fiberglass waste disposal cart. Bullets chewed into it as he dived for cover.

Bolan's mind spread out as his body compressed behind the cart. There weren't many options for him in terms of cover, unless he wanted to race across ten feet of hall and receive a torso-full of enemy autofire. Even with his own body armor, the combined fire of three rifles would probably cut through his protection, and a stray shot could always strike him in the head. The cover he was seeking was away from the three remaining gunmen, and Bolan wanted to get closer to the killers.

He glanced at the wheels of the cart, then hurled his shoulder against the contraption. Suddenly, he had a tank to hide behind. It was only made of fiberglass, and filled with garbage and medical waste, but it had stopped most of the bullets aimed his way. Guiding the cart with one hand, he swept up the Uzi, spotting one gunner angling around the side of the hurtling garbage container. Bolan aimed low, firing just below the guy's waist and riddling him with a half-dozen Parabellum shockers.

Folding over as if he was stabbed in the groin with a hot poker, the terrorist let out a scream, his weapon shifting from laying down fire on the Executioner to blasting out divots of tile and concrete from the floor. With a second burst, Bolan ended his suffering with a blast of slugs that smashed through the top of the shooter's skull, tumbling the would-be killer backward.

Suddenly the garbage cart came to a stop and Bolan's foot skidded out from under him. He came down hard on his knee, grunting at the reflex jolt against his joint. The rolling fiberglass container surged against him now, trying to grind him under. Someone was on the other end, putting a stop to Bolan's improvised tank, taking advantage of leverage and muscle power.

The Executioner pushed himself out of the way of his former mobile barrier, pulling his Desert Eagle in one fluid fast draw. The thug shoving the garbage cart was off balance, with nothing stopping him from tumbling forward.

Bolan helped him with a .44 Magnum coffin nail through his throat.

That left the Abraham's Dagger gunman, and he was nowhere to be seen.

The Executioner braced himself for an even tougher fight.

CRANE SOZE WAS impressed with how fast the mystery man took down the three hired hands. Soze ducked into a room as the inverted tug of war with the garbage cart was going on.

Passing a sleeping patient, Soze threw open the window and clambered out onto the ledge. He'd need to get behind the big soldier, and that meant taking a wall-crawler express. Not the safest or sanest way to travel, he noted as winds whipped at him, but Crane Soze was an expert at trailing suspects from rooftops in dense-packed third world cities where ledges were wide and ornate and buildings scrunched tightly together. He scurried along the ledge three rooms down, snaked through a window and drew his handgun.

"Soze, get out of there," he heard Steiner whisper over his earphone. "We're not going to lose any more people against Geren and her team."

Soze remained quiet, pressing his cheek to the door. He hooked his finger into the wire of the earpiece and popped it free so he could devote his full attention to what was going on in the hallway beyond. Fingers squeezed tightly around the grip frame of the Heckler & Koch USP in his fist.

Steiner gave one more tinny cry over the earpiece, then went quiet.

Soze was glad the soft-spoken, sad-eyed assassin wasn't a whiner over the radio. He had an opportunity to take out Geren and her allies, and he was going to take it.

The Abraham's Dagger fighter stuffed the handgun back into its holster and gripped his AKM assault rifle, keeping the muzzle pointed at the floor. He cracked the door cracked open and he watched the big, dark shape of the soldier pass around a corner. Soze slipped into the hall, feet moving softly on rubber soles. He'd crossed half the distance to where he was sure the mysterious American had disappeared when a sharp hiss sounded behind him.

"Stone? Stone, you read me?"

Soze whirled and dropped into a crouch, taking cover behind a medication cart, taking quick mental inventory of his surroundings. It was a woman's whisper. Tera Geren was behind him, and on the other side was the man in black. Not a good place to be, he realized, but at least he knew where one enemy was, which was more than what they knew.

There was no whispered answer, but Soze wasn't expecting the other to give away his position. He gripped the AKM tighter, scanning over his shoulder. His tendons were taut like mousetrap triggers, muscles ready to snap at the first sight of prey. Heartbeats thundered in a spot just behind his ears, neck throbbing with each pulse of blood that roared through his arteries like jets on takeoff. He was in fight or flight mode, as physiologists and psychologists called it. Knuckles cracked as he gripped the hardwood of his rifle, and he clenched his eyes shut for a moment, hoping no one heard the ever so subtle sound of his joints snapping and loosening up.

Death was close, and it was going to explode on this hospital floor.

Gunfire suddenly chattered.

"Shit!" he heard Geren curse. Bullets blasted from her position, and Soze was on the move, slipping around the corner, rifle leading the way. He glanced back in time to spot a man in black. Cold blue eyes bored down on him, the face a craggy mask of controlled fury, long, lean limbs propelling him forward.

Soze whirled, trying to raise his rifle to saw the big, grim bastard in two. A burst of rifle fire peppered the walls, but stopped cold as a big hand smeared in ebony greasepaint clamped over the barrel and halt the swing of the weapon. The Israeli wasn't a small man himself. However, the Abraham's Dagger fighter didn't see the sense in wrestling for the control of a rifle.

He brought up his forearm, blocking a punch from the big mystery man, releasing his shooting grip with his other hand. Soze rocketed a knee that caught the big man just above the hip. The American grunted with the impact but didn't release the rifle, instead bringing the frame of the solid weapon up hard into the head of the outlaw Israeli.

Head swimming from the cuff of the rifle, Soze stumbled backward, out of the tall wraith's grasp, making it seem as if the blow had taken more out of him than it really had. Dropping against a counter, he coughed and wasn't surprised when his own blood dribbled from his lips onto the mottled gray surface. Blinking away stars, he waited for a burst of gunfire to cut him down, but his gamble that the enemy wanted him alive for questioning was paying off with each tick of the clock.

He let his feet slip out from under him, going down to his knees.

"Nice try," the American growled, digging his fingers into Soze's collar.

The Israeli acted immediately, arm snaking around the tall man's leg, and with a surge of strength, he stood up hard, knocking the man off his feet, spinning with lightning speed to bring his boot down in a murderous stab to the American's vulnerable throat.

8

Mack Bolan was no Superman, and he never claimed to be flawless. Instead, like a certain contemporary of the fictional comic book hero, he preferred to be prepared when the worst hit. That meant having a harness full of utility pockets and pouches full of equipment, weapons and ammunition to cover dozens of treacherous contingencies.

It also meant that he knew how to react when the bottom fell out and his enemies were pressing their attack. As soon as Bolan felt his balance going, he allowed his muscles to loosen, going from spring hard to soft and relaxed, his only muscle contraction, jamming his chin to his chest so that as his shoulders smashed into the floor, his skull didn't bounce off unyielding, merciless tile. As it was, the impact knocked the breath from him, and his head rolled back, hitting the ground much more slowly than it would have had he not tucked in tight. In the same heartbeat as the Executioner went down, Soze rose to his feet, knee hiking against his chest to cock a kick aimed toward the floored soldier.

The Executioner slapped the floor and surged against the ankle of his attacker, his body rolling over the sole point of balance the man maintained while his other foot clipped Bolan's biceps. Hot warmth flushed under his sleeve as the savage kick split tape and skin, popping stitches in one brutal broadside. Bolan wrapped his arms around Soze's knee and got to his own knees, shoulder rising and jamming against the Israeli's crotch.

The renegade commando wasn't standing still for it, and Bolan felt explosions go off in his skull as fists impacted on his head. Punches rolled off the heavy, curved bone protecting his brain, but sooner or later, those impacts were going to cause him some serious trauma. Bolan snapped himself erect, driving Soze up and over the counter at a nurse's station. He didn't let go, listening to the man grunt as his spine barked against the edge of the countertop. Soze twisted viciously, fingers snapping out and clawing toward Bolan's face.

A finger raked Bolan's cheek, raising a welt. He backed away, releasing his foe's leg. The Israeli was off balance on the counter, giving the Executioner an opening. A swift one-two punch hit Soze in the sternum and jaw, sending him tumbling, almost comically, backward.

Bolan reached for his Desert Eagle, drawing it before finding himself in the path of a sailing chair. He sidestepped most of the hurtling missile, but a padded fiberglass arm still struck him in the shoulder, jolting him. Staggered, the Executioner tried raising his Desert Eagle again, getting off one shot at a lunging blur.

Soze grunted as a 240-grain hollowpoint rolled off his Kevlar body armor and one broken rib. His hot breath poured over Bolan's face like rancid water. The two men crashed across the hall, a tangle of arms and legs. Bolan's wrist was being held at bay, the muzzle of the .44 Magnum pistol bobbing up and down. The perverse struggle surged on as first the American, then his Israeli foe, rolled on the tiled floor.

Bolan let go of the Desert Eagle, twisting his hand around

to claw at Soze's forehead. The close-shaved scalp didn't give any hair for the Executioner to use as leverage, but his fingers scraped down his opponent's forehead, one finger managing to gouge into his eye. There was a flinch, a natural reaction to optical invasion, and with that brief weakening, Bolan had his advantage again, grabbing a chunk of collar as he burst from Soze's grip. With a twist, he yanked the stocky renegade's head from the floor, then rammed his other forearm under his jaw and bounced the Israeli's head off the tile.

Soze's whole body jerked as his head rebounded into Bolan's plunging fist, dropping back to the floor with an ugly dull thud. The ex-Mossad commando hooked his fingers into the armhole of Bolan's combat vest, then twisted, driving his knee up into the soldier's stomach. With the double leverage, Bolan found himself flying headfirst into the wall. Only by twisting with every ounce of agility he had did he avoid concussion or a neck injury. His already blood-soaked arm and shoulder left a dark, glistening smear on the pale paint.

The Executioner rose to his feet, arm surging with a twinge of pain from ripped skin and bruised muscle. He grabbed the wounded limb and looked back at the brushstroke of his lifeblood left on the wall. Soze glanced at the dark streak and smiled.

"You're going to have to be pretty good if you think you're gonna beat me single handed," Soze said and chuckled. He started with a lunging side kick that Bolan took on his left forearm, grunting under the impact.

Soze dropped to the balls of both feet, dancing in tight, fists launching like lightning. The Executioner backpedaled along the hallway, slapping and deflecting the Israeli's punches with both hands, keeping his bloody bicep out of reach, but using his forearms to soften and disrupt his enemy's salvo of blows.

The Executioner's heel struck an overturned cart, and he stopped, forearms pumping to block more and more punches as Soze let go with another flurry of strikes.

"Nowhere to go?" the Israeli asked.

Bolan snapped his left shoulder forward, hard, taking a solid punch and feeling the bruise already forming. It hurt like hell, but the Executioner snaked his ankle around the renegade assassin's foot. His right fist swung around, catching Soze just above the kidney. Bolan's second strike was with his left hand. Fingers curled into hooks of steel-hard flesh tore through the eyebrow and cheek of the other man's face. Blood sprayed freely.

As the Israeli howled in surprise and shock, the Executioner followed up with a palm-heel stroke that struck the dead center of the murderer's face.

Soze was sent stumbling, heels skidding on the floor as he fought to maintain his balance, arms windmilling. There was no mercy from the Executioner as he moved in. He grabbed the Israeli's web belt and hauled him into his knee. Like an understuffed mattress, Soze folded over the stabbing joint that plowed deep into his abdominal muscles, sending shock waves of force rippling through his guts. With a twist, Bolan sent the Abraham's Dagger terrorist flying to the floor, landing in an uncontrolled sprawl.

The Executioner stomped his boot down hard on Soze's arm. He was rewarded with the sound of splintering bone and the high-pitched squeal of agony that signaled a breaking of spirit as well. He clawed his micro-Uzi out of its harness and aimed it directly at Soze's face.

"You have four more extremities left. Three of them will hurt just as bad as that arm. The fourth will set you free from all that pain," Bolan promised in a graveyard voice.

"Pull the trigger. You're not getting anything from me," Soze said defiantly.

Bolan glared at the downed man, knowing that anyone could be broken in interrogation, but he also knew that his team wouldn't have the time to waste on a long interrogation, let alone the risk of having a professional in their midst making every effort to escape. It would make for an indefensible situation.

And still, the Executioner wasn't willing to drop the hammer on an unarmed, wounded opponent, no matter what.

Heartbeats pounded in his chest, ticking off slices of time that in his hyped-up condition could have been seconds or hours. Bolan's head throbbed from the abuse heaped on it in the course of battle. Movement surged in his peripheral vision, and he swung up, Uzi following his line of sight. His vision sharpened on two men with AKs, hurling themselves into view, their weapons tracking him.

There was no more time to contemplate the man from Abraham's Dagger. Bolan took a diving leap backward, 7.62 mm slugs tearing through the air. His Uzi bucked and spit, ripping a fireball as he dropped to the ground, breaking his fall on one bruise-covered forearm. The wild spray of autofire he launched had tagged one of the Taliban recruits, a row of slugs stitching the gunner from shoulder to navel in a wild grouping. It wasn't the prettiest shooting the Executioner had ever done, but it was a controlled, short burst, despite his decidedly uncontrolled footing. On one elbow and braced, he swung the muzzle of the micro-Uzi on the other killer, tripping the trigger once again.

The second burst was equally short, five rounds flashing from the end of the barrel. Not a shot from the salvo missed, and the combined impact knocking him off his feet in a messy display.

Bolan remembered the body armor the gunmen with Soze were wearing just as the pair stirred, recovering from their shock. One gunner was truly wounded, his arm hanging limp where a slug sliced into unprotected flesh and bone. He clawed desperately to get his rifle with his other hand. The second gunman was getting his feet back under him, spraying a wild burst into the ceiling as he struggled to shoot and stand up at the same time.

The Executioner threw himself prone and saw Soze slip around the corner and disappear into a hallway. He let his opponent escape, instead lining up the ring front-post on the Uzi pistol and ripping a short blast into the bearded features of the Taliban veteran who shot first. Bolan rolled to one side as the injured shooter let go of his burst of rifle fire.

A storm of autofire filled the air before Bolan could get a head shot on the second killer, and he rolled, looking behind him at a Middle Eastern man. He looked more like a Mediterranean Arab than a local native, and he was holding a short-barreled AK-47, looking wildly between the floored soldier, and the Taliban gunman he'd just chopped to pieces.

Bolan glanced back at the enemy shooter. It didn't matter how good the body armor was. The steel-cored 7.62 mm Soviet-style ammunition launched from the AKs was capable of defeating all but the heaviest "bulletproof" vests. The expatriate Taliban thug's Kevlar wasn't thick enough to stop the chest shredding power of the AK.

Bolan turned his attention back to his savior, who stood glancing between him and a figure around the corner.

"Your friend, Tera?" Bolan asked. His grip was uneasy, one hand slicked with blood, one bicep throbbing with pain from the opened wound. He still would have been able to put a dozen rounds into the gunman's center of mass.

"You could say that," Geren's voice called from around the corner.

Bolan lowered his Uzi pistol and struggled to his feet. The Arab man stepped forward and picked up the Desert Eagle, handing it to Bolan butt-first. Up close, the Executioner recognized the man's face. His brow furrowed.

"Haytham is a friend of yours?" Bolan asked Geren.

"You know who I am?" the Hamas man asked.

"You've got a rap sheet. Unfortunately, I've got an armed killer running away," Bolan said. "You're helping us hunt Abraham's Dagger?"

Haytham nodded. "I'll help you."

"Forgive me if I don't shake your hand right away," Bolan replied, heading off in pursuit of Soze. A broken arm wouldn't slow the man much, but it would hinder his ability to fight back.

"Laith?" Bolan called.

"I'm reading you, Colonel."

"If you see a man nursing a broken arm, that's our Israeli. I want him alive if possible. For a long talk."

Laith chuckled over the headset. "One kneecap, coming up."

Bolan turned the corner and realized that Soze had cut through the center hallway of the building, probably to get to the other side. He turned back and raced for the stairwell on the other side of the building. The door was swinging shut as he reached it, and he slammed his right shoulder into it, bringing a flare of new agony down his injured arm. He didn't release his death grip on the Desert Eagle, though, and slid through the door, going down the stairs, following the racing stomps of rubber-soled boots on concrete. The echoing drumbeats raced up like panicked doves in flight. The soldier's pain disappeared with each bounding leap down the flights of steps, his long legs allowing him to clear to landings in only a few bounds.

He was taking a bruising as he hit the bottom of each landing, and the scrape of his guns against the brick was definitely giving his position away. But the Executioner would rather take the heat of a bullet than allow anyone else to get hurt.

Almost on cue to that internal admission, a trio of gunshots barked up the stairs, bullets whistling past Bolan's head to smash brick and drop broken chips into his hair. Bolan ignored the stinging splinters of stone and raised both guns, firing the Uzi until it was empty. The Desert Eagle issued only two meaty roars. There was a strangled cry below, and Bolan continued down the stairs, leading the way with the Desert Eagle, wobbly in his right fist. There were three more shots left in the gun.

Soze wasn't moving, his Kevlar was wet and sticky with blood, the side of his neck drenched in dark crimson. The Abraham's Dagger man glared at him through enraged blue eyes, gasping with pain and weakness.

"I'll give you medical attention," Bolan told him.

"You'll give me shit," Soze grunted. "You don't have the time to interrogate me properly. By the time you do, we'll get everyone else we're looking for."

"Says you," Bolan challenged. He stayed three steps up, away from the downed assassin. "We can do this the easy way, you know."

Soze still had his gun clutched in what was once his good hand, but both weapon and hand were drenched with blood.

"Both my arms are dead to me, American," Soze whispered. "And you know my face. But you're not going to get anything more out of me."

Bolan took a step forward, but the assassin kicked out. He winced as he slid down the bare brick of the stairwell. More blood pumped from the neck wound.

"It's possible you'll let me bleed to death, or into unconsciousness more likely," Soze whispered. "But you have one small problem. I'm willing to die for my beliefs. Are you willing to die for the children of terrorists, Mr. Bleeding Heart American?"

Bolan looked at Soze's other hand, the hand of the arm he'd broken. A small egg-shaped form lay in the palm, a pin dangling from a ring around the man's thumb.

"Four," he began to count.

The Executioner whirled, charging back up the stairs.

"Three..."

One landing up was not enough room to get away from the concussion and fragmentation of the blast.

"Two..."

Bolan leaped like a cat, clearing a second landing. He spotted Haytham and Geren on the stairs above him. He started to speak, to warn them of the grenade, but instead he ran. Dropping his pistols, he grabbed their shirtfronts and shoved them down hard against the thick, sheltering shields of the staircase.

"One..."

Crane Soze ceased to exist as anything resembling a human being. His body was dismembered by the awesome force of 6.5 ounces of high explosive. His legs were intact, but his torso and head were obliterated.

Up two flights, Bolan and his companions were feeling like God Himself had reared back, bringing down His fist upon their bodies. No shrapnel had rebounded and struck any of them, but the concussion wave was another thing entirely. It was a massive, hateful beast that took them and chewed on them until they felt like their stuffing would pop out of their skin. Once more, Bolan's head thundered from overpressure shock in a confined space.

But he would live. His vision was already refocusing, and as he pulled himself to his feet, he realized his balance was already returning. Equilibrium preserved, he checked on the others.

Neither looked to be in the best of health, but then, neither looked dazed and bewildered.

"Colonel?" Laith called.

"Laith, forget about picking that last guy up," Bolan said. The earplug on his radio set had saved his hearing in that ear.

"What happened?" Laith asked.

Bolan sighed.

"He went to pieces."

MARID HAYTHAM DIDN'T know why he chose to enter the hospital to aid Tera Geren in the rescue of the UN worker. He radioed his status to the rest of his team. His mind was racing.

The gunfights, the presence of two enemies of his organization and his people, the conflicts of loyalties churned in his gut. He stepped past the shattered remains of Crane Soze, the heavy concrete of the landing buckled by the grenade's-explosion.

"I'm sorry we didn't get a prisoner," he said softly, bending over the dead man, fingers poking at the corpse.

"We don't have time to stick around," Geren said sharply. She looked like a person trying to sit comfortably on the edge of a sword. Her voice was taut and hard, and she didn't give the impression that she was going to take much playing around.

Prodding the hideous mess, Haytham knocked loose a wire that came over the shoulder of the smashed remains. The big soldier bent over the dead man, gripped the microphone cable and tugged. The Palestinian saw what he was doing and gripped whatever was worth holding and hauled the bloody mess forward, exposing the back-mounted vest pouch for a radio system.

"Just like on the vests we borrowed from them," Bolan explained. "Except this will have the radio frequencies they're working under."

"They'll change it all," Geren spoke up. "They'll know his body was captured."

"They'll assume the radio was destroyed when the grenade went off," Haytham said. "Not protected by a foot and a half of flesh, bone and Kevlar."

The tall man plugged the earpiece from his own radio into the captured unit and listened. He didn't stop walking, and Haytham and Geren both followed silently, as if drawn by some powerful magnetic charge. He led the way down to the bottom of the steps, still paying attention to the radio, eyes scanning the stairwell.

He unplugged the radio unit and stuffed it into his vest, reconnecting to his own LASH. "Laith, anyone responding to the gunfight in the street yet?"

"Not yet," Laith responded. "But I hear them coming."

"We're at the first floor now," he said.

Haytham paused. "I cannot join you."

Geren and Bolan came to a halt, both looking at him.

"We're on the same side, as rare as that might seem," Bolan stated.

Haytham had seen the ability of the soldier. The man before him was a hardened warrior. Even with one arm drenched with blood, he was still standing tall and firm, while Haytham's hands trembled from the aftereffects of the grenade detonation.

The Palestinian was surprised at the soldier before him, a total lack of accusatory anger in his features. Ice-blue eyes peered deep into him, regarding him, taking a measure that Haytham actually felt ashamed that he might not live up to. The man was a Westerner, but there was something…bigger about him. He was a force unto himself, like the living, walking embodiment of an ideal that was asking for more than just an arm's-length alliance for the time being.

"We'll trade cell phone numbers," Haytham said quickly and softly, feeling ashamed of himself to pass off his chance to stand tall beside this stranger.

"That'll work," the American said.

Relief washed over Haytham, a relief he didn't understand. By all rights, they were men who would be at each other's throats at any other time. Instead, it was a truce, two enemies uniting against a common cause. Haytham memorized the number given by the big man in black, then gave his own information.

Geren looked between the two of them, similarly bewildered by the awkward, unusual, but solid détente that her companion had established.

"Peace between us for tonight," Haytham said, offering his hand. "For tomorrow, we may return to the sword."

There was a moment's pause.

The American man put his finger to the earpiece as Laith's voice was audible over the tiny speaker. "Colonel, we've got company on the way."

"We hear you," Bolan answered, then shook Haytham's hand.

The soldier's mitt was huge, making Haytham feel childlike. A melancholy wave washed over his features. "I would hate to see you as an enemy tomorrow," he said.

The wraith spun and disappeared into the shadows, Tera Geren hot on his heels.

Haytham dumped his AK in the stairwell and took off into the night, pulling his battered old army-issue jacket tighter around himself to fight off the sudden chill running through his body.

THE LAND ROVER'S ENGINE turned over easily for Robert Wesley as Geren and Bolan scrambled into the back seat. He glanced at them in the rearview mirror.

"Who'd you meet up with?" he asked, and the two shared a conspiratorial glance. A long moment's quiet hung uncomfortably in the air like a cloud of acrid smoke. Wesley drove slowly past where Laith had parked himself, so slowly that the young Afghan warrior was able to throw open the door and pull himself inside without the American driver even needing to tap the brake.

"That's a good question," Laith responded. "What's going on here?"

"Hamas is in town, and they're looking for Abraham's Dagger," Bolan told them. "We met a more…moderate member of the group who felt that working alongside us was better than working against us."

"One member?" Laith asked. "Explains how he slipped past me."

"That and there's a half dozen entrances to the hospital," Wesley replied. He glanced to the back where Dr. Mikela Bronson sat, eyes wide with bewilderment as she rode in darkness with four heavily armed strangers who had claimed to be on her side, her protectors against an unknown death squad that had pursued her and her friends across half a continent from the Mediterranean to a shitty little hospital within spitting distance of Pakistan.

Any doubts she held were gone with the first gunshot through the window what felt like years ago. In reality, it was less than twelve minutes by his watch. Wesley's heart was slowing, but there was still the occasional sharp tang of adrenaline that spiked through it, branching out and down his arms, lighting him up like a Christmas tree with nervous energy. He desperately wished he'd brought a pack of cigarettes with him, but he knew better than to bring a load of coffin nails on a mission. Instead, he pressed his molars hard against one another, brow furrowed with worry.

"Wake up, Robert," Laith said. "Unless you want me to drive."

"Sorry," Wesley answered.

"What's troubling you?" Bolan asked.

"Just worried about the doctor," Wesley told him. "Are you all right Dr. Bronson?"

There was a short, nervous nod. Her creamed coffee-colored features seemed even paler now than when he first saw her, but he wondered if it was just a trick of perception played by his mind.

"I guess so," she voiced a moment later. There was a soft tremor to the words, and he could see her knuckles pressing the skin across them tight to the bone as she hugged her vest to her.

"You're in good hands," Bolan told her. "And the men who are trying to hurt you will be stopped."

Mikela's big brown eyes flicked to the Executioner's craggy face. His voice was soft, yet filled with the deep timber of resolve. He wasn't making a hollow promise.

When he spoke, Wesley suddenly found himself believing with his whole being that the frightened healer tucked in the third row of seats of the Land Rover was going to be safe from what vile howling armies of the damned Abraham's Dagger could summon. Doubt burned away and his jaws loosened some.

"Thank you," Mikela answered. The tremor of fear was

gone from her voice, and deep within Staff Sergeant Robert Wesley's heart of hearts, he felt a tremendous debt of thanks to the tall stranger who soothed the hearts and minds of innocents caught in the cross fire.

9

Greb Steiner watched the Land Rover disappear. Even though his rifle had the range, he wasn't sure he had the power to punch through the roof of the vehicle. It was festooned with layers of gear and assorted flotsam in an obvious attempt to blunt any effort to shoot through the roof with all but the heaviest of rifles. Even if he could penetrate the big SUV's top, he wouldn't be able to hit his target because he didn't know where she was.

He wished for a moment that he'd brought along a rocket launcher, but then he wouldn't have gotten into position as quickly.

He blamed himself for not being able to put a bullet into that terrorist-coddling bitch's back when he'd had the opportunity. A mere second sooner on the pull, and she would be dead, and Soze wouldn't be lost.

It didn't look like the enemy had captured his compatriot, which meant that Soze was dead.

He wouldn't have had time to talk, and from the sound of the explosion inside the building, he might even have chosen to take any secrets to oblivion with him. Steiner fought off a wave of mourning agony and tossed his rifle across the divide to another rooftop. He'd go on foot, far less obvious, back to Abraham's Dagger. He didn't want to broadcast anything over the radio in case they had captured Soze's.

If they were smart enough to take down his partner, they'd be smart enough to get whatever was left of his gear to try to track them down.

Steiner reached the street in time to catch sight of a lone, beardless Arab man. Instincts tingled at the base of his skull and before he realized it, his hand was wrapped around the grip frame of his SIG-Sauer P-228. He hadn't drawn the gun, and it took every ounce of will he had to pull his fingers from the handle.

Instead, he scrunched his head down between his shoulders, his beard billowing up and almost covering his mouth. He settled down as he realized he recognized the man.

The world of Israeli vs. Palestinian terror and counterterror was a close, insular one, and the best of one side knew who the best of the other side were.

Marid Haytham was one of the enemy's best. He also was all but untouchable by Abraham's Dagger because he was the sole survivor of his family—killed by a helicopter rocket attack on a Palestinian police station. An antitank rocket missed the police station and landed right in the middle of Haytham's kitchen while his wife and three children were preparing dinner. Haytham survived only because he was hunched over the hood of a battered old car in his garage, trying to get the most out of ancient oil filters and spark plugs.

Since then, Haytham had waged his own war against the Israeli military. It wasn't the same kind of fight that was waged by his fellows in Hamas, but he was still a killing machine when it came to soldiers. He'd engineered the destruction of five of seven helicopters from the air base that launched the assault on his home, killing three pilots and injuring dozens of flight technicians and other pilots in a mortar assault.

He went on record, taunting the Israeli government to quit

being cowards and murdering bystanders and fight like men. This didn't make him popular among his bedfellows, but it earned him some respect from the counterterrorism community. Steiner, however, felt like the man deserved everything he got for throwing in with the murderers of children.

The idea of the "noble savage" had never appealed to the sad-eyed Israeli. These were Israeli lands, not stolen territories, and the unbathed, rotten-toothed primates who dared to seek recognition as humans had no right to bitch when God's chosen were finally back in the land of their birthright. Steiner's eyes narrowed as he watched Haytham, revulsion churning inside him.

It would be so easy to take aim and blow Haytham away with two shots to the head, but that wouldn't be enough for Steiner. It had to be close, and it had to be with the .22 that was his signature. He had chosen the little gun because it was a symbol of what he felt about his enemy. They weren't worth a real gun—they were pests, rodents to be plinked at and eliminated with a couple of barely audible pops to the skull.

Something else stayed Steiner's hand. If Haytham was on the scene, that also meant other Hamas terrorists were present. Killing the Palestinian would mean that he couldn't get hard intel on the new enemy running them down.

It was bad enough that Tera Geren had added to the ranks of her hunting party. Now a second pack was added to the chase. And with the loss of Soze and twenty Taliban mercenaries to date, avoiding ambush and assault was going to be as much a problem as seeking out the UN relief workers and killing them. He fingered the cold metal frame of his radio and contemplated contacting Rhodin. The risk of Geren's group hearing him was high, but if he didn't use the frequency that Soze set his radio to, he might get away with a short message in case things turned to shit.

"Dagger Two to Dagger One. Double bad news to report," he called.

"Dagger One, reading you," Rhodin's voice answered.

"Keeping it brief. Dagger Five has gone home. The doctor went away on a house call. And we might be having ham for dinner too," Steiner replied. He hoped his cryptic remarks were clear enough, ham meaning Hamas.

"Fuck a duck," Rhodin growled.

"No time. I'm going on a walk, you know dear?"

"Wait—" Rhodin began, but Steiner unplugged the radio and stuffed the earpiece into his pocket.

"You know dear" was the pronunciation of a military acronym—UNODIR. Unless Otherwise Directed. It was what Abraham's Dagger often did when they checked out for a night to keep their activities in the dark from the Mossad. It wasn't the most foolproof means of slipping off a short leash, but it gave the covert killers a sense of lung-filling freedom.

Steiner followed Haytham, trying to control thoughts of murder until he could get some allies on the scene.

MARID HAYTHAM FIGURED OUT he was being tailed by the end of his fifth block of travel. He didn't head back to his shot-up gold-colored Peugeot immediately after leaving the hospital. He preferred to approach his vehicle once he was certain nobody was shadowing him, or observing him leaving the scene of a gun and grenade battle in a hospital.

The tail was good, but Haytham was a man who lived on a razor's edge, having been hunted for three years by the best that the Mossad had to throw at him. He kept walking, leading the tail through a maze of alleys and streets, cutting between buildings when he had the chance. But the hunter seemed to have almost superhuman senses, anticipating his every effort to double back and race for his vehicle.

While Haytham had a Makarov in his pocket, with three spare magazines of potent 9 mm ammunition, he knew a fresh gunfight wasn't in the cards. Not when he already saw the few police cars from the town assembling at the scene of the previous battle. Making a lot of noise would have only drawn the local cops down on him, for questioning at best, or a chestful of rifle slugs at worst.

Leaving Abraham's Dagger free from retribution.

Haytham owed his children and wife that much. He clenched his eyes shut, fighting off a wave of tears at the thought of them, trying to slide a wall of ice between his emotions and his conscious mind. It was hard, but as the seconds passed, and the sting of sorrow burned away, he was clear headed and dry eyed.

His hunter stood at the end of a gangway between two buildings, watching him, eyes squinted in cold rage. It took a moment for Haytham to realize his efforts to get his mind under control had cost him his lead, but the hunter was holding back.

Naturally, Haytham thought. You want me to lead you to my comrades.

The enemy stood rooted, glaring, hunched against the cold Afghan night as much as he seemed braced against a wave of revulsion and fury. Perhaps it was body language, or some other subtle sense, but Haytham could feel the anger crawling down the gangway, tendrils creeping through the shadow like wisps of frosted mist, reaching for him, touching him and sending an brittle tingle of unease through his entire being. He had never bought into so-called psychic phenomena, but this night, looking at a man he knew with dead certainty was from Abraham's Dagger, he could see how two minds could be linked across a hundred feet.

With a deep breath, Haytham sidestepped around the corner and raced up the street. Each step ate up ground, cutting the distance between him and his bullet-pocked Peugeot. He glanced back, but his enemy wasn't coming out between the two buildings. His spine tingled with fear. If he wasn't being chased, that only meant that the hunter was running a parallel course.

It was a mistake using a recognizable car like the Peugeot again, after hard contact with the enemy. It was covered in bullet holes, which marked it as being present at the scene of another battle. But the Hamas team had few enough vehicles, and he wasn't going to be allowed another. He'd have to make do.

Stealing a new car would be problematic. Few Afghan citizens owned vehicles. Few enough government officials even had vehicles. The Peugeot was as precious as the gold it shared its color with, whether or not it was defaced by the savage wrath of an AK-47's broadside.

So far, all he knew was that his enemy was on foot. The Palestinian tore through the night, with not quite reckless abandon, but as fast as he could without losing track of the man on his tail. He hated the fact that he had to turn and run, but he remembered that moment, that second of total contact with the hunter, the feeling of cold dread threatening to strangle him.

This wasn't the place to wage his fight, not if he was going to have any chance of hunting down the rest of the Dagger cell in Afghanistan.

His car came into sight as Haytham made one final turn. He stopped, scanning up and down the road. His fist filled, unconsciously, with the Makarov pistol, fingers squeezing so tight on the steel he felt he could almost bend the metal in his bare hand. He looked back, then he checked both ways up and down the street, seeing no sign of his assailant. In a mad dash, he charged the final fifty yards to his car, stopping only to unlock the door. He glanced back and saw the Abraham's Dagger assassin come around the bend, a black looming shape that made Haytham's heart stop. Two blocks away, at the hospital, Afghan and coalition military were assembling, investigating the gunfire and grenade explosions. Just exactly the kind of crowd that he wanted to avoid getting into a gunfight near.

He shot a glance back toward the Israeli, but he was gone, a shadow lost among the darkened nooks and crannies.

The hunt was over for the moment. Haytham pulled himself into his car, fired up the engine and pulled slowly away from the curb. No one stopped him, and the Abraham's Dagger killer might well have been a ghost for all the evidence left in his passing.

It was a draw.

But he'd have his chance against the mad dog Israelis.

Blood would flood the streets the next time they met.

It DIDN'T TAKE LONG for Captain Blake to show up at the safehouse, but it was as cordial a visit as it was a surprise.

Blake arrived with three Green Berets in full battle dress. Bolan recognized two of them as Jerrud and Montenegro, but wasn't sure about the other. The Executioner bristled at the thought of coming into conflict with soldiers on the same side. He was certain that there were at least three more Green Berets in position, with full fields of fire and the firepower to blow the little house to hell in the space of a heartbeat should Blake decide to write off these intruders.

There had been enough of a gap between the fight at the

hospital and Blake's arrival for Bolan's companions to clean off their greasepaint, attend to their wounds and change into fresh clothing. Bolan had traded his blacksuit for a set of dark tan BDUs, which would serve as a decent set of street clothes for the frontierlike streets of Afghanistan and still allow him some stealth. He had a black sweater packed away in his war bag, along with his guns and other gear.

"Captain Blake, welcome," Geren spoke up. Her voice dripped with sweetness. Bolan could sense the effort she was putting into remaining calm. "To what do we owe this pleasure?"

Blake only glared at her as he passed by, closing the distance to Bolan until they were nose to nose. The captain's pale hazel eyes locked like lasers onto Bolan's, the pupils tightening to pinpricks, amplifying the red cracklike veins around the corners. The Executioner could smell a hint of alcohol on his breath, though the man stood steady and sober, unwavering and unslurred.

"What the fuck do you think you're doing blowing the hell out of a goddamn hospital, you psychopathic fucking cowboy?" Blake snarled.

"I didn't," Bolan answered simply. Hopefully, if he played his cards right, he wouldn't provoke Blake any further. He regretted the necessity of a raging battle through a building full of bystanders. That it was a hospital full of sick and injured, and the good men and women devoted to helping heal them only made it more difficult.

"Don't give me this crap. I just came from the hospital. Seems there's a bunch of Taliban veterans in varying degrees of dead," Blake explained. "Including one guy in a stairwell who had a grenade dropped on him, conveniently obliterating any chance of identifying his corpse."

"I didn't drop a grenade on anyone tonight," Bolan told him

truthfully. He hoped that honesty was the best policy. Bolan had learned long ago that using ninety percent of the truth was the most effective part of role camouflage.

Blake's eyes narrowed. "Then could you explain a shoot-out near a burned down garage earlier today? I have command on my ass about all these dead bodies suddenly dropping out of the sky."

"I'll claim responsibility for that," Bolan said. "I'll even claim responsibility for dead gunmen at the hospital. I didn't use a grenade. I don't endanger civilians if I have a choice. And if they are threatened, I don't hide my head in the sand and claim to be following orders."

Blake's eyes widened to the point where Bolan thought they'd pop out of his skull. Shock froze the man's face. He finally recovered his senses, turned and stepped away from Bolan.

"Who else was with you?" Blake asked, voice harsh from the struggle to contain the fury within him.

"Just me. I went to see Dr. Bronson. There was an attempt on her life, and I fought my way out of the area, bringing her to safety with me," the Executioner explained.

"You're making my life very difficult right now, Colonel Stone," Blake snarled.

"That wasn't my intention," Bolan answered. He never intended to interfere with the work of lawmen or anyone fighting the good fight. But a soldier's duty was to protect his country. Bolan's sense of duty expanded far beyond simple nationality, though, and that often brought him to cross-purposes with those who just had a job to do.

Blake glanced back at him, breathing deeply to try to keep himself calm. "So where is the doctor now?"

"She's in safe hands," Bolan answered. This was where he was going to either completely sever ties with the Special

Forces team or find out how far Blake was willing to go, how much he was willing to bend the rules.

"Where?" Blake repeated.

"You aren't on my need-to-know list, Captain," Bolan told him. "She's in safe hands."

Blake looked at Geren, voice straining, cheeks reddening. "Do you know?"

The woman shook her head. "I honestly don't."

"And where's Laith Khan?" Blake asked. "That little smart-ass—"

Blake spun, glaring at Bolan. "You sent them off together."

Bolan remained impassive. He had his answer about Blake's compliance.

"I can't believe how arrogant you are. You come into my area of operations, you start a shooting war that is piling up an enormous body count, and now you're kidnapping noncombatants?" Blake asked. "Who do you think you are?"

"Someone who's protecting those noncombatants. If I hadn't been at the hospital, that team would have killed dozens of people to cover up the murder of Dr. Bronson, perhaps after they tortured her," Bolan explained. "I saved lives tonight."

Suddenly, the rage drained from Blake's face. It was as if he'd blown out the connection between his emotions and his body, all that remained being a simple automaton. "Arrest this man," he said to the Green Berets.

Bolan shook his head. "We don't want that."

"Take him. We're going to put him in the stockade," Blake said.

Bolan sighed. This was what he'd hoped to avoid, but being a consummate soldier, he was always prepared and ready to act. He crossed the distance to Blake in one step and grabbed him by his combat vest, swinging the captain in front of him like a human shield. The three soldiers brought up their weapons at the sudden flash of movement, but swung the muzzles of their rifles up at the ceiling when they realized any gunfire would perforate their captain.

The Executioner took advantage of their pause. Lifting Blake off his feet and using him as a battering ram, he threw the captain against two of the Special Forces soldiers before swinging a kick into the groin of the third Green Beret. He'd learned long ago that surprise was an advantage that could not be matched in any combat scenario. It was the one weapon that never ran out of ammunition.

Geren moved to act against the Green Berets, but Bolan shook his head. He needed her to stick with their plan.

He'd need someone who was still on speaking terms with the local military forces, even after alienating Blake and his Special Forces team this way. Bolan snaked his arm around the head of the man he'd kicked in the groin, grabbing a fistful of web belt.

Blake and his two men were rising fast, and the Executioner swung the stunned Green Beret, boots crashing across the chests of the charging men and stopping them in their tracks. With a flip, Bolan dropped his burden on one of the soldiers with a meaty thump. A sidestep brought his elbow hard into the face of another American soldier, a stunning blow that set him up for a second strike that impacted under the man's ear, sending a shock wave through his central nervous system.

Felled with the blow, the soldier dropped out of Bolan's way, leaving only Blake, clutching his chest, blocking his escape. Not that the Special Forces captain could do much more than accept a punch in his stunned state. Caught on the point of the chin, Blake's head snapped back, shock doing the rest in dumping the man on his back. Bolan stepped over him, crossing to where he'd stashed his war bag.

Geren rushed at him.

"Make it look good," she said as she took a swing at him, her fist bouncing off his freshly redressed biceps.

Bolan winced at the sloppy punch and returned one of his own, regret filling him for the fact that he had to lay out four soldiers on the same side. Geren went down with the punch, but he wasn't aiming to hurt her.

"Sorry," he repeated, again as genuinely apologetic as he was to Blake for disrupting his operations. He scooped up his war bag and grabbed a smoke grenade from its depths.

The Executioner pulled the pin and rolled it out the door, watching the thick, choking mist spit out the top of the canister, the heavy smoke spreading quickly along the line of its path. Once it obscured enough of the area between the door and the car, he plunged into the cloud, heading directly for the Land Rover, remembering exactly where it was parked in relation to the door. Bolan's mental map was correct. He arrived at the big vehicle's door, threw his gear inside and got behind the wheel. The windshield puckered as a bullet went through it, and the Executioner dropped his head, tromping on the gas as he spun the Rover in reverse.

More gunfire chased him, but the Green Berets outside weren't aiming to kill, only to force Bolan to surrender. By the time they realized that they needed to cripple some of his ride's major systems, the Executioner was already spinning toward the road, kicking up dirt to further obfuscate the vehicle's escape. Slugs whined off the ground and the skin of the Land Rover, finding little chance to punch through to a tire or the engine.

He sped away, looking in the rearview mirror as one Green

Beret shuffled out of the smoke cloud, waving dust and chemical smoke from in front of his face. He started to bring up his M-4, and if it had been his intention to kill Bolan, then the ride would have ended right there. Instead, he lowered the muzzle of the rifle in frustration, watching the Executioner do what he did best.

Escape from those who meant to curtail his War Everlasting, and return to the business of hunting down the enemy.

10

Laith Khan's voice was cheerful over the telephone after Bolan told him about the brief scuffle with the Green Berets.

"Sounds like it was fun," Laith said.

"I thought you liked Americans," Bolan said.

Laith chuckled. "I don't like sticks in the mud."

Bolan sighed. "I don't think there's enough mud in this part of the country for Blake to get stuck in."

"Figure of speech, big guy," Laith replied.

"Just try to remember, he wouldn't be here if he didn't care," Bolan answered. "He's trying to do a job, and his hands, unlike ours, are tied."

"Sorry," Laith apologized. "You're right."

Bolan scanned for enemies on the roads or on rooftops. "You're forgiven. Any word on the gold Peugeot?"

"Aleser had a couple of runners come into town to look for it, and they've been reporting in," Laith answered. "You're not going to go meet with Haytham and his boys by yourself, are you?"

"Don't worry, Laith. You'll get as much action as you can handle if my reckoning is right," Bolan explained. "Besides, Dr. Bronson needs someone to watch over her. You're it. I'll go through some of the alternate hideouts for the Taliban holdouts you gave me," Bolan told him. "Something might shake loose if I rattle hard enough."

"And if not?" Laith asked.

Bolan measured his response for a moment. "Consider it incidental pest control."

THE TOP LEVEL of the old Soviet military base had been burned, blasted and looted dozens of times over in the years since the Russians' withdrawal from Afghanistan. The lawless aftermath of the occupation had left those facilities vulnerable to savage assaults. Whatever still stood was so thoroughly defaced by an angry, liberated people that the Executioner barely recognized the facility at first.

Only one building still stood after the hammering of RPG shells and grenades and whatever explosives looters could find to try to pierce the walls. The squat little bunker entrance was pockmarked with the remaining rage of an impotent horde trying to crack open the reinforced concrete and steel frame of the building. Bolan had always admired the old USSR's ability to make cheap and easy items that also could stand up to untold amounts of horrific abuse.

Nothing short of a nuke going off right on top of the bunker would have made a dent. Instead, the Executioner looked for an alternative entrance. The Soviets would not have allowed themselves to be trapped in an underground cavern without at least a secondary exit, one that was well concealed, but still easily accessible to someone who knew his way around such a facility. Bolan had seen his share of such dens of secret warfare across the course of his career. He also knew that without much variation, the architecture of such underground tunnels was a set pattern. Perched on a hill overlooking the burnt-out old Soviet war base, he mentally tracked a spiral out from the central blockhouse, sweeping the ground for the back door.

He spotted a pile of stones that was just a tad too regular to be the natural result of the landscape. It was outside the perimeter of the old base, and had one broad, flat stone large enough to cover a hole a man with a full pack could slip through. Bolan stuffed his binoculars away and shrugged into his battle gear. He tested his arm, the dressing and stitches holding this time. He wouldn't have help dealing with the injury should someone open it up again, not with the immediacy that he'd had at the hospital or with Tera and her first-aid kit.

Crossing the distance to the entrance, he took a quick mental inventory of his situation, not so much in guns and gear, but in what he really had going for him. The Desert Eagle and the Uzi pistol were known quantities, and he had enough ammunition to get him through all but the fiercest of firefights. What Bolan really wondered was whether this side trip was a wild-goose chase or stalking a solid intelligence source. He knew that behind him, bridges burned all along the way, he'd left what little intel the Green Berets had, even though Sergeant Wesley had given him as much as he'd known.

It was a godsend to have Wesley on hand. Bolan was glad the young staff sergeant had been easily convinced to head back to report to Blake on his own before the captain came to chase him down. Not having the young man on the scene had made it easier for Bolan to successfully fight his way out.

It was over now. Bolan was a hunted man, with all hands against him. He wasn't a part of the system and pretending that he was brought him in too close to others, threatening their lives all too often. When it came time to stalk, he preferred to fight alone, no matter how much easier it was to have someone at his back.

Bolan's musings ended as he knelt next to the concealed entrance of the underground bunker. Sure enough, a sheet of almost flat rock was attached to a hinged steel plate. His fingers found the latch. It would have to be a simple mechanism, though sturdy. He down to get a better look at it, illuminating it with his filtered flash. It wasn't locked, but it was secure. It took some effort to get the lever to operate for him, and he skinned his knuckles, but he ignored that and continued on. A few abrasions were nothing compared to the aches and pains he'd been put through over the past couple of days.

He found a darkened tunnel leading down into murky depths. His L-necked flashlight sprayed a pool of red light into the blackness, but there was nothing to see except the rungs of a ladder. Bolan swung his legs over the edge and crawled down onto it, pausing only to examine, then close the hatch behind him. No wires were attached to the hinges, and no alarms sounded below. If there was an electric eye, then his presence would have tripped alerts throughout the complex.

If it was even occupied.

Bolan finally reached the floor. He dropped soundlessly, crouching. Ahead, around the corner, faint light brushed across a wall, a dim glow that made it possible for him to navigate the hallway, cluttered with old crates, drums and cardboard boxes. Stepping carefully to avoid tripping and raising a clatter, he snuck toward the hallway's intersection, ears straining for the sound of any human presence. His fingers screwed a sound suppressor on the threaded barrel of the Uzi pistol with an unconscious, trained ease.

Any gunfight going on in the narrow confines of the underground tunnels would make the one in the stairwell with the Abraham's Dagger terrorist seem like a cakewalk. The suppressed machine pistol would keep his hearing from being temporarily overloaded in a fight. It wouldn't guarantee stealth, he realized, but it was better than nothing.

No sounds reached his ears, and Bolan swung around and continued into the half-lit halls.

The scent of cigarettes and food hung heavily in the air. A thick cloying garlic scent that stung the back of Bolan's nose informed him that people had been here recently. The looters who had thrown themselves impotently at the trappings of their former oppressors were not likely to have come down here, but the more patient Taliban would have found the way, especially with information brought over by rich expatriate Arabs and Yemenis who would have bribed former Red Army engineers who knew the inner workings of such sanctums.

The smell of a cigarette grew fresh and sharp. The pungent odor assaulted Bolan's senses and he slowed. The murmur of two men talking wafted to him on the trail of the scent. It was coming from a doorless room on one side of the tunnel, twenty-five feet down. The Executioner flexed his hand around the Uzi pistol, making sure the grip safety was fully depressed, the chatterbox ready to rip out its payload. It was a faster gun than Bolan would have chosen, but he was an expert at using such machine pistols, and knew how to tap off a short spurt of lead instead of burning off half a magazine with a single pull of the trigger.

Bolan was eight feet from the opening when he heard a chuckle from within, and a shadow fell across the entrance. A soldier in BDUs, with a full beard, puffed on a cigarette. He stepped out, laughing and adjusting his pants. He turned away and walked with purpose. Bolan figured the man was heading to empty a full bladder in the bathroom, leaving his partner or partners alone.

The mercenary paused and started to turn back just as Bolan reached the archway.

Their eyes locked.

The Taliban militiaman's hand dived for the pistol on his hip, and the Executioner ripped a slashing line of 9 mm slugs across his torso, knowing that stealth had been blown to hell.

IT WAS LATE at Hal Brognola's office at the Justice Department. He was the official liaison between the President and Stony Man Farm, the country's top covert antiterrorism operation.

A phone call broke Brognola's concentration on some paperwork laid out in front of him. He took the receiver off the cradle and was greeted by a familiar voice.

"Hal, I need to talk to you."

Brognola knew the drill when the Man called. "Not over the phone," he replied.

"Of course not," the President said. "My driver's waiting out front for you."

Brognola felt his stomach twist. He poured a handful of antacid tablets into one palm and swallowed the chalky mass after chewing them for a minute. He grabbed his coat, knowing full well that when the President asked to see him in person, it meant that there was some snag out in the field. He thought of the missions of Able Team and Phoenix Force, and knew that nothing they were working on should be cause for a quick high-level debriefing.

By the time he'd shrugged into his coat, he was at the front door, briefcase in hand, and saw the limousine driver waiting for him.

The driver handled the D.C. traffic with a silky smooth ease, but Brognola expected nothing less. The limo glided through the rear security access to the White House, and the driver rolled up to the set of out of the way doors that Brognola had long ago named the Civil Servants' Entrance.

The Secret Service guards relieved Brognola of his Glock 23, his snub-nosed .38 Smith & Wesson and the Buck pocketknife folded in his front pocket. Although he was a regular fixture at the White House, Brognola never took offense at being disarmed when meeting with the President.

Some people had to do their jobs all the way, or they couldn't do their jobs at all.

Mack Bolan was one of those people. Few things would ever stay his hand, and Brognola was glad for that.

"Hal, whenever I see you, you always look so lost in thought," were the first words he heard upon entering the office that was reserved for their briefings. It was small, sparsely adorned, but most importantly, it was secure from prying eyes of all forms.

"Part of the job, sir," the head Fed answered. "Is there anything wrong?"

"I'm not sure," the chief executive responded. "Have a seat."

Brognola sat, not quite comfortable seated before one of the most powerful men in the world. It wasn't a matter of being overwhelmed by the importance of the office, or the Man himself. But when things came face-to-face like this, it meant something was shaking and rattling through halls of power that Brognola could only hint and guess at.

"Do you have anything going in Afghanistan?" the President asked.

Brognola's poker face didn't quite kick in fast enough. He'd promised Bolan that he wouldn't interfere in his mission to take out the murderers of a group of relief workers, and now, he was going to be taken to task for something that was starting to break out of control. "There's no official Stony Man presence in Afghanistan," he said.

"But Striker isn't an official part of Stony Man," the President stated.

"I can't lie to you about that. He is his own man," Brognola explained. "When he sees something that has to be done, he doesn't play around with sanction. He steps in and takes whatever action needs to be taken."

"And that generally involves putting a lot of, how do they say it these days, boot to ass?"

"Yes, Mr. President."

The Man leaned back, rubbing his thumb across the point of his chin, eyebrows furrowed in intense concentration. "Have you been keeping track of what Striker has been doing?"

"He's been keeping off the radar as far as I can tell," Brognola answered truthfully. "He's under no obligation to report to me. Why?"

"Because I have two complaints about a situation going on over there."

Brognola felt like he'd been punched in the gut, but a gentle hand was raised to wave off any recriminations. "Nothing that might compromise the Farm, Hal."

"Then what?" Brognola asked.

"The Joint Chiefs have been bickering with the CIA over the presence of an operative in the area, interfering with peacekeeping efforts in northeastern Afghanistan, along the Pakistani border. The CIA is claiming innocence in the matter, and for once, I'm inclined to believe them. The style of this alleged interference doesn't fit a Company operative," he explained.

"Lots of dead terrorists, with little or no collateral damage?" Brognola offered.

"You know Striker better than I do, but even that much was obvious to me."

"The military isn't going to accept any last-minute legitimization I can pull out of my hat," Brognola replied.

"I don't think Striker will be wanting that any time soon. It seems that a Special Forces captain tried to throw him in the brig."

"He'd better have brought the whole A-team with him," Brognola said.

The President laughed. "No. Only half a team, according to the report that crossed my desk."

"Why would this have come to your attention? Aren't there people lower on the totem pole who could be unruffling feathers between the Pentagon and Langley?" Brognola asked.

"There are, but I also have someone who is working for me helping unruffle another set of feathers," the Man answered.

"Whose?"

"The United Nations was asking for help in the investigation of who killed a bunch of their people over there in a refugee hospital. The CIA is trying to stall having the FBI add their brains to the investigation, the military says it's keeping things under control and doesn't need any help, and the provisional government is too busy worrying about warlord infighting to give much concern to a bunch of Westerners blown up by a squad of kooks," he explained. "It's a Gordian knot over there, Hal."

"I figured that much," Brognola responded. "And one where Striker is all alone."

"He appeared to have an entourage of allies on the scene. And he's disappeared now, with an all-points bulletin out for his arrest," the Man said.

"Good luck to them if they want to catch him. He's eluded far more skilled hunters before. He's eluded the entire U.S. intelligence apparatus on his own," Brognola replied.

"You don't have to remind me. I'm under pressure to do something to satisfy the UN, without stepping on a lot of tender toes out there, Hal."

"You're going to make Striker your official response to the hospital attack?" Brognola asked.

"Do you have a better idea? I can tell the UN representative, quietly, that I have someone already on hand," the Man said. "And I can help him out…"

"Striker won't want help, and if you have to start applying pressure to agency heads and generals, the UN will wonder about what you're doing," Brognola said.

"So…"

"Keep everything confidential. The murderers will be brought to justice."

"You act like that's a given," the Man answered.

"Striker will keep fighting to his dying breath to stop those savages," Brognola told him. "You have my assurance this will be settled."

"And everyone else?"

Brognola stood, collecting his briefcase. "Sir, if they get in his way, then I feel sorry for them. I truly do. If they're killers, they won't last a moment. If they're well-intentioned good guys, he's still going to steamroll over them and make them feel embarrassed and bruised."

THE MAKAROV ROUND DUG into the Executioner's chest, slamming home with the force of a fist. The Kevlar armor spread the slug's penetrating force but didn't spare the shock of impact. Bolan took a diving slide to the ground, even as the gunner who'd first spotted him tumbled backward lifelessly. Two men were scrambling in the room as Bolan dived past the entrance. He recognized the little alcove as a mess hall.

He also saw that the two Taliban mercenaries were reaching for heavier hardware than the pistols on their hips, although one of them had the presence of mind to have already filled his hand with a gun.

Bullets zipped over the Executioner's head as he was already at ground level. The gunmen were reacting to where the big black shadow had been. Bolan didn't make that mistake. Aiming just a little ahead of where the running shooter was headed, he ripped off a burst that took the terrorist just above the hip. A salvo of four 9 mm Parabellum rounds punched through soft viscera, exploding the flesh of the gunman's kidney, then tunneled through relentlessly ripping a ragged exit wound.

With a scream, the pistol man collapsed to his knees, but his partner had reached his AK-47 and whirled. Bolan's dive for cover was almost complete as he skidded along the slick stone floor, and he rolled up tight into a ball, saving his legs from being chopped and splintered by a hail of 7.62 mm shockers.

Bolan heard the mad rush of feet, and knew that the rifleman was going on the offensive. He had one opportunity to take the man out without testing how well the Kevlar he wore could stop the armor-piercing powers of the steel-cored COMBLOC rounds. He scrambled to his feet, and timing it perfectly, grabbed the barrel of the AK the moment it poked out the doorway ahead of the rifleman. With a powerful twist, the Executioner dragged the gunman into the hall with him, his foot snapping into the shin of the shooter.

The man shouted in pain, but held on to his rifle, despite the fact that Bolan twisted it, levering the trigger guard now against the man's index finger. Another hard yank and bone snapped. The Taliban fighter tried to cry out, but Bolan cut him off with a breath-stealing punch to the stomach, the power of the blow increased by the unyielding steel barrel of his Uzi.

The thug coughed and gagged, barely able to think before

Bolan swung the barrel of his own rifle hard into the man's face, the merciless wood and steel tearing his cheek down to the bone. The gunner's head bounced back, mouth slack and eyes glazed from the impact. Bolan swept his feet out from under him, letting him crash to the floor, still holding on to the AK.

He pressed the muzzle of the silenced Uzi pistol into the man's face.

"How many more are there?" Bolan asked.

Boots stomped in the hall behind him, and the Executioner knew that the time for conversation was over. He left the staggered gunner where he lay and kept his fist tight around the barrel of the AK, knowing he might need some extra firepower if things got too hectic. He set down the Uzi pistol long enough to scavenge three magazines from the unconscious rifleman. He penetrated deeper into the tunnels, taking a quick left when he saw shadows converging at an intersection over a hundred feet ahead.

The Executioner found himself in a storage room, drums stacked up against the far wall. He squinted in the darkness and saw the international symbol of "flammable."

Fuel drums.

He heard the clatter of boots, lots of them, getting closer.

11

It wasn't the first time that Tera Geren had been punched, and it probably wouldn't be the last. Neither was it the first time she'd been in hot water with agents of a foreign power. Captain Jason Blake was seething and Geren was certain that the swelling red mass on her cheek, puffing her eye closed, was the only thing slowing the Special Forces team leader's desire to throw her in handcuffs.

"That son of a bitch," he growled.

"Tell me about it," she answered. "I fix up his arm, give him a nice bed to sleep in, and he coldcocks me and steals my Land Rover."

Blake looked like he was about to say something, but Geren had maintained enough angry tension in her voice to give a convincing impression that she didn't like Bolan's plan of action. Then again, she *didn't* like the big soldier's idea to head off on his own to limit collateral damage. She didn't mind the shiner that was hard and tight, forcing her into a one-eyed squint.

"It's your own fault," Blake grumbled, steering them through the streets of Chaman.

Geren was shocked by the comment. "What gives you that idea?"

"Working with someone like him. I've heard rumors about a guy like that."

"Colonel Stone?" she asked.

Blake shrugged. "If that's what they're calling him now. There've been half-remembered names circulating through the community about him."

"I've worked with him, and I know him. He doesn't mean any harm. If he did, you'd be sporting bullet holes, not bruises," Geren explained.

Blake snarled at the reminder, but his features softened. "I know that. He didn't return fire. He probably had more fire-power than the specialists I brought with me, and he didn't fire a single shot."

"So why can't you call off the hunt for him?" Geren asked.

Blake frowned. "It doesn't work that way."

"No?"

"He isn't part of the system."

The Israeli agent rolled her eyes, feeling her head swim at the effort. "Screw the damn system. Nobody talks to each other from different groups under one government, let alone allied governments. That's how so much shit happens. Nobody's willing to listen to someone else from a different set of stupid letters."

Blake sighed. "You would know something about that."

"That's why Israel is still standing. We do have most of our shit together. Sometimes it doesn't go right, and the boss on top feels that it's better to drop a whole neighborhood to get one man. But at least we have a network that is a network. People work together because they know that if they don't, people are going to get dead. We're not perfect. But dammit, we try, and someday cooler heads are going to prevail, but until that time, we still have bad guys to put down, and this particular time, the bad guys also happen to be renegade Israelis."

"What?" Blake was hit with a palpable wave of shock.

"A death squad calling itself Abraham's Dagger is on the loose here. They're after the witnesses of a refugee slaughter in a camp called Shafeeq. Dr. Bronson was one of those witnesses," Geren explained.

Blake took a deep breath. "Let me guess—the one with the grenade?"

"Blew himself up before leaving us any clues to lead to his buddies in the Dagger," Geren said.

Blake frowned. "You were there?"

Geren kept quiet.

"Damn it, Rosenberg…"

"Tera," she corrected.

"Tera, you're going to have to come clean with me if I'm going to help Colonel Stone."

"He doesn't want you involved."

Blake stared at her. "What?"

"He doesn't want any American soldiers involved. He doesn't want me involved. He doesn't even want his Afghan guide involved, and the only reason he hasn't completely ditched Laith is because he isn't fluent in the local dialects," Geren explained.

"That's suicide—" Blake began, but his attention was attracted by something up ahead in the road. Geren snapped her head around to catch the glint of light from the rising sun, reflecting off drab metal, worn smooth by peeling paint, yet not quite rusted.

"Rocket attack!"

Blake stomped on the gas, accelerating ahead as rocket-propelled grenades suddenly sizzled forward, riding rails of smoke toward them. Geren tensed, wishing Blake hadn't confiscated her weapons for the trip back to headquarters. Three rockets were flying all at once, and all three missed them as

Blake powered the Mercedes past their point of aim. She spun in the shotgun seat, watching as the two Humvee escots behind them were turning hard and breaking formation, plowing through feeble fences and down through roadside ruts.

"Grab my M-4 from the back!" Blake shouted.

Geren didn't argue, slipping into the back seat and grabbing the Green Beret's rifle and spare ammo. The short-barreled weapon was easy to turn and hammer into a rear passenger window, the squat aluminum tube of the adjustable stock providing all the punch necessary to knock out the safety glass. She flipped the gun like a baton and poked herself halfway out the window, triggering bursts where the contrails of the rocket launchers were still dissipating.

A scream emanated from the rocket exhaust cloud where her bullets met flesh. Wild return fire swarmed, muzzle-flashes illuminating in the rusty dawn light, smoke and dust providing sharp contrast to the starbursts given off by chattering enemy rifles. Geren left it to Blake to keep them driving fast and hard, and she selected a cluster of enemy weapons and she fanned the group with an extended burst of her own.

The sweep of autofire drove the enemy gunmen to cover, but heartbeats after the autoburst, in the middle of changing magazines, Geren was forced to duck back into the Mercedes. The road and the door of the vehicle were being hammered by return fire.

"Blake?" Geren asked as the Mercedes jerked to one side, still roaring up the road, passing the line of ambushers who were being torn to shreds by twin lines of fire from the Humvees. Knowing the two vehicles that were with them, she almost pitied the ambush squad, being slammed by automatic 40 mm grenades and .50-caliber slugs that would tear a human being in two with ease.

"I'm okay. A bullet got through the door but glanced off my load-bearing vest. I don't feel any blood," Blake said.

Geren kept an eye out. More riflemen were off to the other side, hastily struggling to get their RPG up and firing at the Special Forces convoy. She aimed, holding down the trigger for a long blast of 5.56 mm slugs that sailed into the second ambush squad. Men twisted and screamed. An RPG shell popped up into the air like a bottle rocket before spinning lazily to slam into the earth with a ground-shaking eruption. But the squad of gunners were undaunted by the Israeli's autoburst.

Not that it mattered. She'd spoiled the aim of the grenade attack, and now the Special Forces Humvees were at an angle on the road to see the gunmen. Again, twin streams of heavy weapons fire slammed into the pocket of Taliban militiamen. She saw that individual Green Berets were adding their rifles to the fusillade of withering fire that chopped into human flesh, though that was like adding the effects of a squirt gun to a fire hose. Bodies were smashed to a pulp by explosions or slugs.

Geren shuddered at the carnage, but doubled her discomfort as she realized that this had all taken place in the space of a few seconds, less than a minute of actual time.

It never ceased to amaze her how quick and sudden death could be.

She looked back to Blake.

"Captain?"

The Mercedes gave a violent shudder. It felt as if gravity had let go. Geren's fingers released the rifle and grabbed for a handhold somewhere in the interior of the vehicle. She was flung toward the ceiling of the upturned Mercedes, and a heartbeat later—backness.

IN THE BLACKNESS of the shadow-laden storage room, the Executioner was pulled in tight, ready to repel any and all invaders with whatever means he had. He had a war bag full of his usual combat gear, and a confiscated enemy rifle. He also had years of combat experience and a knowledge of the way the human mind worked. Hands feeling in the shadows, he found a row of lockers with his shooting hand and swiftly moved along it feeling for a possible gap behind them. Finding none, the bank continuing flush against the wall, he groped the handle of one then another locker until he found one that was open. The fit was tight, but there was no upper shelf. That made it possible to squeeze his frame into the cramped space.

He tugged the locker door almost completely shut as he heard the stampede of boots rumble past the storage area. A flashlight swept the room, and Bolan remained still, watching the shaft of light play across the interior. After a few moments, the overhead lights in the room came on and three men rushed inside, looking around.

The men scanned the place quickly, thinking that the best hiding spots were deep within the room, instead of glancing back to the corner. Crammed in the locker, Bolan didn't have the ability to move quickly, but tucked deep into shadow, he was almost invisible. As the men looked around the storage area, so did he, following their movements through the vent slits, taking inventory as they moved boxes and crates.

It was more than just a fuel dump, and there was enough gear to wage a whole new war. Bolan waited, seemingly for an eternity as the trio of Taliban mercenaries poked and prodded boxes and barrels before finally turning and racing out of the room.

Bolan was about to move when he caught the sound of more boots at the entrance, and heard a curt order. The overhead lights went out, and the stomping boots thundered down the hallway as the guards separated, seeking out the Executioner in their midst.

Bolan slipped out of the locker as smoothly as he could and drew his red filtered flashlight. The short cycle of red light didn't travel far or show up in even moderate lighting. The red lens filter allowed him to see things at the space of about ten feet with crystal clarity while making him less noticeable, even if waving it in absolute darkness.

He didn't really need the torch to find the bit of shelving he was looking for. He remembered its location from when the lights had been on, but he didn't want to trip over anything and make a sound. Reaching the crate, he set down his light, took off the top and found what he was looking for. A box full of riot-control gas grenades. In the tunnels, they would be as good as gold, but only as long as Bolan could protect himself from the ravages of the choking clouds.

He hadn't seen any gas masks, but he did see a box of goggles. He pulled some electrical tape from his vest, sealed off the vent holes in the sides of one set and strapped them around his head. He crouched down as he heard a couple of men jog past, then disappear. Bolan wasn't about to go searching for something to replace gas filters. He removed a wad of gauze from his first-aid pouch and taped it across his chin and the bridge of his nose.

It was time to let the Taliban know that their reign of terror was going to end in tears.

MARID HAYTHAM SAW the Special Forces convoy take some bad hits after wiping out two groups of ambushers with their superior firepower. He knew full well the effectiveness of RPG-7 Soviet-designed rocket grenades, having used them in everything from laying vengeful waste to an Israeli airfield to taking out troop trucks and armored personnel carriers. The Mercedes in the lead took only a glancing blast, being the quicker, smaller target. However, the slower, larger Humvees were smacked with relative ease, even by the horrible Taliban marksmen.

Haytham looked at his partners, Fasood and Sariz. "We have to do something," he told them.

"Like what? Fight off men armed with rockets?" Sariz asked.

"The woman in the Mercedes is our best chance to track down the men from Abraham's Dagger," Haytham stated.

"A temporary alliance, you mean?" Fasood asked.

"With them?" Sariz asked. Even Fasood looked doubtful.

Haytham hit the accelerator, racing past the shattered hulks of the two Humvees. A Taliban gunman spotted the speeding automobile, a hard worn Russian ZIL, and shouted a warning as Haytham took the vehicle off-road, plowing through two of the mercenaries before they had time to dive for cover.

Fasood pointed the muzzle of his submachine gun out the window and he held down the trigger. The Hamas man was one of the few people who Haytham worked with who had actually trained to control his weapon and put bullets on a target. Two Taliban men were cut down by precision gunfire from the Palestinian shooter. Their corpses spun out of control to the ground as their life forces were cut from them.

Haytham exited the driver's door and fired off rounds from his Makarov, taking enemy gunners in the heads and chests. When his weapon ran dry, he ducked down, pulled his rifle and rolled free of the car, certain that Fasood was doing the same maneuver on the other side.

Sariz snarled in angry derision at the choice that Haytham had made, but that didn't keep the Uzi clamped in his big fists from rattling off an extended blast of slugs that served only to keep the enemy's head down. Scattering the remaining fighters of the ambush team was not a waste of ammo, for the time being. Haytham simply raised his Uzi as Sariz's auto-fire herded gunmen into his line of fire and ripped into them with salvos of 9 mm slugs. Using the hood of the ZIL as cover, he kept up the pressure, Fasood's weapon chattering on the other side.

No return fire came, and Sariz finally stepped out of the ZIL, giving a howl of victory, emptying a quarter of his magazine into the sky before Haytham gave him a hard shove.

"What's wrong?" Sariz asked.

"Gravity, you nit!" Haytham scolded.

"What?"

Haytham grabbed the man's shirt and yanked him back into the cover of the ZIL, moments before the steel roof came alive with the sounds of leaden rain as gravity pulled the 9 mm bullets back down. The dirt was alive with impacts, and Sariz howled in surprise.

"Who's shooting at us?" he snapped.

"You! Bullets go up, and they come back down," Haytham growled.

"Gravity," Sariz muttered. He looked out and saw Fasood, clutching one arm, scowling at the men in the car.

"Twit," Fasood shouted. He took his hand away from his shoulder, wet and glistening with blood, then looked around. "We'd better get the woman."

"And the man," Haytham replied. "I'm sure that whatever happened, they called for help as soon as the first shooting started."

"I thought you wanted some kind of alliance," Sariz said.

"We'll be friendly, but we'll be friendly on our terms, all right?" Haytham explained. "I'm not going to have a rifle in my hand and two vehicles full of dead or wounded American soldiers when their backup arrives."

"That's logical enough," Sariz said. "But I still say we'll get more out of her my way—"

"If she doesn't help us willingly, she's all yours," Haytham allowed, to dismiss his arguing and get to work.

The three Palestinians raced to the battered Mercedes. They found Captain Blake and Tera Geren within, both still breathing, both bloodied, but starting to move. Haytham pointed the muzzle of his Uzi at Blake's face and shook his head.

"We're not going to hurt you, but I don't have time for you to make a scene. Join us in the ZIL, and we'll get you back to your people," Haytham said.

Blake's eyes blinked slowly, as if covered with a film of gum that impeded their process. He slowly crawled out of the shattered windshield of the car, stopping on his hands and knees at Haytham's side. Fasood dug his fingers into the collar of Blake's combat vest, half dragging the stunned Special Forces captain to the ZIL while Haytham reached into the Mercedes again and found Geren, far less responsive, glazed eyes staring dreamily at him.

"Geren?" he asked. "Are you all right?"

"It only hurts when I breathe," she answered.

Haytham gave a soft smile. "You have to be a lot more cooperative, or my people are going to give you hell."

"Oh God, did you attack the convoy?" Geren asked.

"No, but I didn't want you falling into the hands of Abraham's Dagger."

Geren smiled weakly. "You're sweet for a member of a murderous terrorist organization."

Haytham took her hand and gave a tug. "Did that hurt?"

"No," she said, her wince making the answer less than convincing. Haytham pulled her along anyway, helping her get out of the overturned Mercedes, and to her feet. She wobbled, but she was small enough that she wasn't a burden to Haytham.

"You drive, Sariz," Haytham ordered.

"Why me?" Sariz whined.

Haytham glowered, staring daggers through the man.

"All right. But one of these days—" Sariz began.

"If you finish that threat, you'll be dead by the time the last word leaves your lips," Fasood said, leveling his Uzi.

Sariz glanced between Haytham and his loyal friend and simply got behind the steering wheel.

It was going to be a real game of diplomacy to keep Captain Blake and Tera Geren alive, Haytham realized, but he knew that it was the right thing to do. It didn't make the torment whirling and churning in his soul any smoother, but it was something.

THE EXECUTIONER HADN'T planned on encountering an army in the confines of the underground bunker, and he knew that stealth and guile were, as always, going to have to be his sword and shield in combat with the Taliban mercenaries. To make the most of what tools he had, he'd come up with a plan that had flickered in his mind the moment he'd spotted the air duct.

Bolan found the vent cover in the darkness, and only a few moments with the screwdriver on his Gerber Multi-Tool was necessary to take off the grille. He gathered up a couple of boxes and slashed them open to form a large square that would completely cover the surface.

For what he planned, all he needed was a simple duct tape and cardboard cork. He plucked the pins on five of the confiscated riot-gas grenades and hurled the bombs as far as he could down the vent, listening to them raise a ruckus as they bounced off sheet metal with deep, booming tremors. Gas hissed and by the time the fifth grenade was in, fingers of the noxious gas were trickling out around the duct's opening. Bolan took a couple of deep breaths through his improvised mask, and was pleased to note that his breath and sweat-soaked swab of gauze was blocking the stinging effects of the noxious cloud. Still, he slapped up the panel of cardboard with its duct-tape border and blocked the air vent. He had turned the circulation system into a bottleneck for the expanding riot gas. He heard cries of pain and confusion down the hallways.

Bolan spun and navigated to the front, filling his hands with the AK-47 just as he reached the entrance to the storage room. Complaints in Arabic carried to his ears, and he paused long enough to use another tear-gas grenade, flipping it into the hallway on a sizzling contrail of pumping irritant. There was a sudden increase in the volume of the complaints, urgency filling voices before they dissolved into choking, coughing and gagging.

It was a golden opportunity. With his enemy blinded and nauseated, they wouldn't be able to spot him among them until it was too late. The battle would be fought on a ground where he had the best footing, the best visibility, and even though the CS gas was bringing a salty sting to his nostrils and the tickle of a cough to his throat through his improvised mask, he was far better off than the men whose sinuses were inflamed and whose throats were swollen tight with the scouring, almost paralyzing effects of the irritant smoke.

Bolan needed a prisoner.

The Executioner exploded into the hallway, parting the chemical smoke and descending upon the hapless Taliban mercenaries.

12

Wael's eyes stung as he staggered through the hallway, arms up trying to keep the burning clouds from savaging and assaulting his face. It was a futile gesture, and he knew that if he had a mask, it would be easier, but there were no such masks just laying around the well-equipped underground compound. Plenty of supplies had been left behind by the Russian devils when their occupation was broken, but it was a crapshoot as to what was to be found where.

He had plenty of ammunition for the rifle in his hands, and grenades on his belt and food to fill his stomach. That was what had mattered ten minutes before when the quiet little bunker was just a place for him to rest his head while the strangers from Egypt were assembling his brethren for an assault on the enemies of Allah.

That was before the gunshots, the alarms, the panicked response to an invader who had penetrated into a supposedly impenetrable bunker.

Wael's tearing eyes searched through the haze that filled the half-lit hallways, each breath like sandpaper through his throat and nose. He was amazed that all that came out was thick, clear mucus and not sticky blood, his lungs burned so thoroughly. He paused as a tall form stepped through the fog, AK in hand.

"Sayed?" he gasped.

The buttstock of the rifle swung up and hit Wael above his navel, the wind forced up and out of him in a torturing blast of breath. He staggered, folding over the strike, and felt an elbow chop down onto his neck. The floor met his face hard. Light flashed inside his skull like a burst of lightning as he curled on the cold concrete floor. He glanced up at the tall figure, chemical smoke swirling around it like it was the center of a dust devil.

Wael shuffled back from the big wraith as he spun, lashing out with a long powerful arm to backhand another of his allies, sending him flying into a wall with a meaty slap and a slow slide down brick.

Two men staggered to grab at him, fingers curled into claws as much in pain as in the need to hook the intruder's flesh. Instead, their hands groped at empty air, the flickering figure disappearing between them. A long leg snapped up, knee striking the rib cage of the first man, a fist hammered into the back of the second man's head, knocking off his cap. Both hat and body tumbled forward to land at Wael's feet.

Wael wondered desperately why he had proved foolish enough to leave college in Yemen and end up in the hands of a living devil who tossed aside strong warriors for Allah. It was as if they were mice, playthings at the paws of a desert hunting cat. With a cry of horror, he watched the tall monster grab another of the Taliban expatriates and lift and hurl him seemingly without effort down the hall.

Bones crunched as the man landed, unforgiving stone and gravity combining to punish him. Getting as much of his will to fight as he could, Wael clawed for the pistol in his belt.

The man whirled, eyes flashing in reflection from the hazy, fogged over lights, then flicked out his hand. Spears of agony plunged into Wael's shoulder, only a bit of his consciousness recognizing the clatter of the AK-47 bouncing on the floor. All he knew was that his clavicle now flushed with the lava heat of a broken bone, his body was twisted in pain, his fingers now useless.

Iron-hard fingers wrapped around his throat, and Wael felt himself lifted.

"How many of you are there?" the voice said in English.

"Please—" Wael gasped, drool pouring from his mouth with each ragged breath. "Please, in Allah's name, I beseech you—"

Wael felt himself slammed hard into the wall, the weight of mountains falling against his chest with the savage impact.

"Allah doesn't care about a rapist and murderer of children!" the man snarled. Wael felt his genitals shrink in horror, his entrails twisting into a tight, cold ball up against his spine.

"Your only hope is to tell me what you are doing here. Tell me why you are trespassing in the lair of the Russian devils."

"We were told to come here by the warriors from Egypt who claim to be the chosen of Allah," Wael whimpered.

"We? How many?" the wraith growled, working on the fears of the injured man.

"There were ninety of us this morning. Now there are but fifteen," Wael sobbed, tasting his own tears.

"Where did they go?" the man demanded.

"Some went to capture a Jewish woman," Wael said, eyes clenched in fear of staring death in the face.

"And the others?"

"They were meant to launch an attack," Wael answered.

"Where?"

"An American base—"

Suddenly, the weight was off his chest and broken collarbone. He could breathe in deep lungfuls of the noxious gas, which now was as sweet as the scent of flower petals in relation to the horror that loomed in his face. His eyes blinked with gummy slowness, but when he looked around, there was no one standing in the hall with him. With a trembling hand, he clutched his shoulder, bending over.

He and his brethren had been spared from the full wrath of an angry god.

For that, he would give thanks to Allah. He looked at the pistol, half drawn, balanced precariously in its holster, then scraped his thigh against the wall, the cursed thing clattering to the concrete. He gave it a kick, casting it away from him.

No more would he bear arms against the other children of God, because he knew, looking into those glassy, round eyes, his punishment for such an act would strike him down like lightning.

BOLAN LEFT BEHIND the injured militiaman, realizing that the doomsday numbers were tumbling out of his control. Abraham's Dagger, realizing enemies stalked its heels, was turning to face its foes head-on. That left Tera Geren vulnerable to a counterattack, knowing that at least one enemy force was out there, knowing who she was, where she was.

"Capture the Jewish woman," the man had said.

Ninety men. Fifteen left behind.

Bolan couldn't even begin to figure how many he'd already encountered. Another twenty or thirty at the least. Abraham's Dagger had to have had an entire army. Passing storage areas, he spotted littered remains of opened crates of weapons, rifles and rocket launchers and grenades discarded next to emptied containers.

He took inventory on the run, pausing only to toss a CS tear gas grenade ahead of him, or to slash the buttstock of his AK across the jaw of any Taliban mercenary foolish enough to stumble, choking, into his path. The trail of unconscious men grew longer, but the clues ahead of him were shortening to a dread conclusion.

The assassins had located the mother load of their prey, and they were going to make every effort to eradicate them from existence.

And Bolan was long behind in the chase.

Bolan flipped open his phone, but the concrete and earth over his head effectively cut him off from communication with the outside world. He was going to have to get to the surface. That meant getting back to the entrance.

The Executioner whirled; thundering feet were racing toward him. Once more, the remaining Taliban mercenaries were mustering their forces to repel this invader, and when they cleared the stinging cloud of gas, they'd have a relatively clear view of him. Pivoting on one foot, Bolan ripped the Uzi pistol and the Desert Eagle from their respective holsters.

Shadows burst through the cloud, hobbling along, some clutching broken jaws, others with their faces contorted in chemical-induced pain, all of them lunging as one single-minded entity. Through their blurry vision they saw a tower of a man, wisps of clouds swirling at his feet, his face an inhuman mask behind a soiled black improvised gas mask with flashing goggles.

"You have the chance to leave here alive," he warned them, fingers resting lightly, but securely, on the triggers of the weapons.

The group paused, the urge to blink away the sting of tear gas dissipating like mist in the sun. A couple glanced at each other, seeking support, seeking advice, trying to decide whether their strength in numbers was enough to overcome the aura of death and dread that surrounded the intruder like a storm.

"Move aside," Bolan ordered.

The group of men parted and Bolan lowered his guns, striding past them. He felt their gaze on him, and though he could smell the stink of his own sweat and breath through the gauze pad, tanged with the extra spice of tear gas, he could smell their fear as well. He'd proved himself to them as something they had no hope of standing against, and in their weakened moment of doubt, they folded completely. Bolan didn't run, and he didn't turn back. He strode through the tunnels to where he came in.

None of the Taliban dared lift a finger to stop him.

If only it would be so easy against Abraham's Dagger, Bolan thought.

ROBERT WESLEY RETURNED to headquarters, realizing that it had grown more crowded by at least twice the number. He also noticed that half the Special Forces team was gone as well.

"What the hell's happening?" he asked Warrant Officer Terrence Ogden, the executive officer of the command post while Captain Blake was in the field.

"Wesley," Ogden said. "Jesus, things have been going crazy over here. Blake went out to pick up that Colonel Stone last night."

Wesley had expected as much, but kept his tongue still, looking around at the newcomers in the command post. From their uniforms, he could tell that they were Marine Corps, and from the lack of name panels and rank insignias, he figured that they were Force Recon or Marine Expeditionary. He raised an eyebrow and tilted his head at the presence of the sudden influx of leathernecks.

"The jarheads came in last night after Blake moved out to talk to Stone," Ogden explained. He took a deep breath, and lowered his voice, leaning closer to Wesley. "We just got an emergency radio transmission about eight minutes ago. We're loading up as many people as we can and moving out."

"What's wrong?" Wesley asked.

"Strap into your combat gear," Ogden ordered. "Blake and the convoy came under fire. We've been trying to raise our people, but there's been no response so far."

Wesley's face drained of blood. "Good God."

He looked among the group. Jerrud and Montenegro had gone with Blake. Those two were particularly close friends of his among the team. "Had they picked up Stone and Rosenberg?" Wesley asked.

"They reported they were bringing Rosenberg back. Stone flattened Blake and the three guys with him, and took off running," Ogden reported.

Wesley tightened his combat vest across his chest and cinched his helmet in place. "This is getting more and more fucked-up."

"No kidding," Ogden responded. "I'm glad you made it. I didn't want to leave this joint to the Marines."

Wesley looked around. "No. We going to have them backing us up on this retrieval?"

"Yeah. Fortunately, we have a strong GPS transponder signal from one of the Hummers, and there's an emergency beacon giving us another signal," Ogden said.

A red-faced Marine wearing mirrored shades stepped up. "You're joining this little field trip?"

"Yeah," Wesley answered. "Staff Sergeant Robert Wesley. Intelligence and heavy weapons."

"Sergeant John Bannon," the Marine said, putting forward a big paw. "Good to be workin' with you."

Wesley accepted the handshake, and the two men headed out to the vehicles.

"How bad is this gonna get?" Bannon asked. "You seem to have an idea what's got the Marines in bed with the Special Forces."

Wesley responded, "Renegade Israelis, Hamas, the Taliban, and to top it all off, a bunch of innocent UN doctors and care workers."

The sergeant took a step when something flickered in his peripheral vision. It wasn't even conscious thought that sent him sailing against Bannon, shoulder striking the man in the chest hard enough to send him flying four feet, both of their bodies knifing through the air.

A sudden flurry of bullets smashed into the ground, kicking up dirt.

The Green Beret looked up at the rooftops surrounding his headquarters and spotted a dozen bodies and a dozen rifles, all looming over them.

"We're under attack!" Wesley roared as a fresh wave of autofire rained down on the Marines and Special Forces troopers.

LAITH KHAN WASN'T GOING to sit still. Not when he had the opportunity to do some good. The colonel had explained that he'd get into enough action soon enough, but the young Afghan didn't think that Stone would mind a noncombat mission of sorts.

Dr. Mikela Bronson, sitting next to him in the jeep, looked skeptical of the Afghan warrior's logic, however.

"Listen, Doctors Koenig and Takeda are going to be fine at Makaki," she told him.

"Just like Sofia DeLarroque and a few dozen coworkers and patients were safe?" Laith asked.

The doctor pursed her lips, her eyes turning to the road in front of them.

"And let's not forget your adventures last night at your supposedly safe hospital," Laith added. "Makaki is a heavily overworked camp, with thousands upon thousands of people living in shanties around it. The camp's security wouldn't notice a strike force until their brains were exiting their skulls at over a thousand feet per second."

"All right!" Mikela snapped.

There was an uncomfortable tension in the vehicle as Laith kept the hammer down.

"I'm sorry," he apologized sullenly.

"You didn't have to describe everything in gory detail."

Mikela's dark eyes scanned the horizon as they moved along. Morning was dawning quickly, and Laith could tell that exhaustion was getting to her. He was about to say something when the phone on his hip warbled.

"Laith, where are you?" Mack Bolan's voice cut over the radio waves.

"I'm heading to Makaki," Laith answered. "The last two witnesses to the Shafeeq massacre are working there."

"I thought I told you to stay put. Is Dr. Bronson with you?" Bolan asked.

"She's with me."

Bolan sighed. "Laith, Abraham's Dagger has at least seventy-five heavily armed Taliban veterans out in force today. Some of them went to capture Tera, and the rest are being given orders to attack other zones."

"You know where?" Laith asked.

"I didn't see any records, and I don't think Abraham's Dagger would be stupid enough to leave anything in writing for me. But my educated guess would be the Special Forces

HQ at Chaman and the camp at Makaki," Bolan said. "And you're going to be rolling right down the throat of an ambush."

"But," Laith began, "you came here to stop the murders of—"

"I know that," Bolan answered.

"So where are you? What are you going to do?" Laith peppered him with questions.

"I'll think of something," the Executioner told him.

The connection went dead and Laith stared at the road ahead of him.

"What?" Mikela asked.

"That was Colonel Stone," he explained. "The men who wanted you dead last night are going to make an assault on the Makaki camp to get the remaining two doctors. And they're going to attack the Special Forces HQ at Chaman. They're also going to capture the Israeli woman who was with us last night."

Mikela's face twisted into a mask of worry. "But—"

"Yeah. It would take hundreds of men for them to do that," Laith stated. "My brother has about a hundred men, but there is no way he could get them to either place in time to make a difference. And if what Colonel Stone says is right, then the U.S. military is coming under the hammer right about now."

"All those people, though," Mikela answered. "There's five thousand refugees at Makaki—"

"I know that," Laith answered. "And those are my people. Afghans. Real Afghans, not some punks who thought it would be some sweet summer vacation to load up on a truck and go shoot some Russkies to get themselves their little paradise."

"I'm sorry," Mikela said. "Is there anything we can do?"

"I just got through talking to the one man I trust to let me know when we can do something," Laith responded.

"Can he do anything?" she asked.

Laith kept quiet, realizing that every second he kept his foot on the gas, winding down the road to Makaki, he was breaking the big man's rules of engagement.

Orders or not, Laith couldn't sit by and let an army of thugs sweep down on his defenseless people.

MACK BOLAN WAS PUSHING the Land Rover to its limits, knowing that the alignment and the undercarriage were taking a pounding even their legendary reputation wouldn't stand up to for long. He had his phone open and was about to dial the number he remembered from Marid Haytham.

The phone vibrated in his palm, and Bolan answered it immediately.

"Colonel Stone?" Haytham's voice came over.

"What's wrong, Haytham?"

"It's Tera Geren, sir," came the answer.

"Where are you? Is she all right?"

"My partners are debating giving you our location," Haytham explained. "But she's okay. Well, she's alive. She took a beating, and so did Captain Blake."

"Abraham's Dagger launched an assault on their convoy," Bolan deduced.

"Exactly," Haytham responded. "Listen, I know we promised a truce between our sides, but the men I'm working with aren't too interested in honoring words exchanged with Americans and Jews."

"And you?" Bolan asked.

There was a momentary silence.

"The Israeli military murdered my family, Colonel. Do you comprehend how it feels to wake up one day and realize the people you love are dead and you were completely impotent to do anything about it?" Haytham asked.

"My father, mother and sister died just like that, Haytham," Bolan stated. "Don't explain to me what loss is."

There was a choked moment. "My apologies."

"You couldn't know," Bolan returned.

"We need to know where Abraham's Dagger is. We have to act against them, it's the only bargaining chip I have available against my partners," Haytham stated.

"Tell me where you are, or get a force up and ready and meet me somewhere neutral. Bring Blake and Geren along too," Bolan compromised.

"Let me try to convince my people," Haytham said quickly. "I'll call you back."

"Right," Bolan said. He was about to shut it off as the connection went dead when the phone shook again, the vibrating ring drawing his attention. "What?"

The sound of gunfire on the other end of the digital stream was all too familiar, Sergeant Robert Wesley's voice was a bellow over the line. "Colonel Stone! We're under attack in Chaman!"

"I know," the Executioner answered. "How are you holding out?"

"Pretty damn bad. They're blowing the hell out of this place, and not giving us a chance to respond. They took us by surprise," Wesley snapped back. "I'd like to blame the Marines for distracting us, but these guys were given good placement, and I don't like speaking ill of the dead!"

"Marines?" Bolan asked.

"Force Recon," Wesley answered. "Colonel Stone, we need reinforcements!"

"I might have some help coming your way," Bolan said.

MARID HAYTHAM TURNED BACK to the eight Palestinians who watched him like hawks.

"Any reason why the Americans aren't answering our calls?" Sariz asked with a sneer.

"I don't know, but Colonel Stone took my call. He sounded like he was in a hurry, but he was willing to meet at a neutral location if you didn't want to talk with him here," Haytham explained, getting out the offer before the balding Palestinian could cut him off.

"You're soft in the head as well as the heart!" Beraz, a burly man over six feet tall, spoke up. "If he comes here, the Americans are just going to—"

"Listen," Fasood spoke up, flexing his freshly bandaged shoulder, "there are as many Americans who are sympathetic to the cause of a Palestine free of Israeli oppression as there are who buy completely into the lies of the Jews."

"That's right," Haytham answered. "This is a man who spoke to me as an equal and with trust. He had me outnumbered last night, and he had more than enough firepower to kill me, or capture me. Instead, we parted under a flag of peace."

"Because he wanted to track you down and kill all of us," Sariz told him.

"I'm getting tired of your mouth," Fasood growled. "It was your bloody bullet that hit me, not anyone else's. You shot me, you twit!"

Haytham saw the group of Palestinians split up. Only one other man, Sellil, stood with him and Fasood, leaving it six to three odds in favor of the hard-core Hamas soldiers. "Fasood, it's all right."

The big man was about to argue, but he saw the look in Haytham's eyes and nodded, cooling down. Haytham tossed Sellil a glance, and he also wordlessly accepted the stand-down.

"I'm going to call Colonel Stone, and we'll take Blake and Geren to another location," Haytham explained.

"The Jew bitch stays here," Sariz snarled. His knife glinted from his fist, a grin splitting his face. "We need to get acquainted."

Haytham rolled his eyes. "I don't have time—"

Something boomed and hissed outside, and Haytham realized he'd never spoken truer words in his life. The time for negotiations ran out as the wall of their hotel suite exploded, black smoke and debris swirling as a thunderbolt-like explosion struck the building.

13

The Executioner followed the columns of smoke burning into the sky on the way back from the former Soviet base, his instincts grabbing him by the gut and dragging him toward the site of a recent battle. The Land Rover jumped over one rut in the road and he saw even more of the asphalt chewed up by what he quickly recognized as the effects of a 40 mm grenade launcher. He kept the pedal to the metal when he spotted two Humvees at roadside. Each of the vehicles was smoldering, sporting gaping holes where smoke poured out.

He skidded to a halt by the closest of the Humvees and got out, dragging his war bag with him, which contained a well-stocked medical kit. He looked around and heard a cry come from off to his left.

"Over here, Colonel!"

Bolan recognized the man. It was Sergeant Jerrud, and he was kneeling at the top of a roadside ditch, rifle at the ready. Bolan raced over.

"Who's hurt?" he asked, kneeling and pulling out his kit. He counted the men. There were only three, and he instantly recognized the one who was wounded as Sergeant Montenegro. Another Green Beret was resting on one elbow, his face a mass of bruises.

"Just Montenegro, sir," Jerrud responded.

"And the others?" Bolan asked.

"Just what you see," came the response.

Bolan knelt by Montenegro, who already had a bandage pressed to the side of his neck.

"Shrapnel, sir," the other Green Beret responded. "Bounced off the clavicle and went through the trapezius muscle. He's bleeding a lot, and he's gone into shock. We've already used our supply of Ringers solution to keep him stable."

"I'm sorry," Bolan said. He was about to do something when the other man reached for the medical kit.

"Sergeant McKorkindale," the medic told him. "I bet I'm a little more qualified than you are. Trouble is, my kit's burning up."

"Go ahead," Bolan said, handing off. "Jerrud, you're pretty much on your own for the time being. The team's HQ is under attack in Chaman."

"Shit on a stick, sir!" Jerrud exclaimed.

"No backup is going to pick you up, and I can move the three of you, if you want."

"That would be good," Jerrud answered. "But what about Blake and the woman?"

"Did you see what happened?" Bolan asked.

"Well, the Tali-mooks were all celebrating having taken us down and were around Blake's Mercedes, when this big black ZIL comes roaring up and a bunch of Arabs pop out and start shooting. If I had more motor controls than to barely crawl out of my Hummer, I'd have thrown in with them, they were righteous shooters" Jerrud answered. "It was two guys who did most of the ass kicking, though."

Bolan wasn't going to ask for a description, but he knew who at least one of the men was. "What happened next?" he asked.

"This bald little prick hops out after the shooting's over and empties his gun into the sky, and the lead dude, a guy with a beard like a local, jams him into the car before the bullets come back down to earth," Jerrud answered. "Asshole ended up clipping the other guy from the ZIL. A big guy, 'bout your height, but about fifty, sixty pounds heavier."

"How'd they treat Blake and Geren?" Bolan asked.

Jerrud shook his head. "Blake got a gun waved in his face, but it seemed more like a matter of formality. Geren? The girl?"

"The one you know as Rosenberg," Bolan said, cursing himself for forgetting Tera's cover for a moment. He tried not to remind himself of Afghanistan splitting at the seams, two bloody rifts being torn open even as he was here in a roadside ditch with an injured Green Beret and the other survivors of an ambush.

"She was treated a little better, helped to walk to the Russian car," Jerrud stated. "Who were they, sir?"

"Hamas," Bolan explained. "It's a long story."

"Hell, I'll believe Captain Kirk and Mr. Spock at this point," Jerrud muttered. "I'm just glad to be alive. And I'll be even more glad if we can keep Montenegro—"

"Quit talking about me in the third person," the big sergeant said. "I'll live."

Bolan sized up the tall man, lips pale and gray, eyes sunken, one arm strapped tight to his side. "I'll take your word for it," he said.

"It looks worse than it feels," Montenegro said.

"That's called morphine and Demerol, dimwit," McKorkindale spoke up. "You're taking it easy."

"Easy isn't in our vocabulary today, gentlemen," Bolan explained.

"We heard," McKorkindale answered. "A man can dream, can't he?"

"Get into the Land Rover," Bolan said. "I'm going to see if I can salvage anything. Did you collect—"

Jerrud held up three chains with plastic encased dog tags. "They're coming with us, Colonel. But please, we have to send someone for their bodies."

"We will," Bolan promised. "We just have to get out of this alive."

GREB STEINER GLANCED at Olsen Rhodin, the sadness having left his anger-hardened eyes. Ever since the previous night, with the death of Soze, and with the escape of Marid Haytham, he had become a changed man.

"I told you I didn't want you making hard contact with the enemy," Rhodin explained halfheartedly.

"Shut up, you spineless bastard," Steiner snarled.

"Listen," Rhodin began, but a hand clamped over his mouth. The stubby finger squeezed on his lower mandible so hard he was afraid the bone would snap like an eggshell.

"You listen," Steiner said. "I've seen this mystery man at work. Suddenly, you get all tail between your legs and are launching all kinds of sloppy attacks. You're attacking Green Berets and refugee camps, and why? Because you're afraid of someone who matches the legend of a devil. I've seen him, through the scope of my rifle. He's human!"

Rhodin shook Steiner's hand away, terror making his heart hammer a mile a minute. "Then if he's human, he's not going to be able to get in our way for the hits on Takeda and Koenig."

The convoy they were in, heading for Makaki, was a dozen vehicles long, but the plan was to abandon the trucks long before they got to the outskirts of the camp. Getting the heavy

transports through thousands of people in tents and improvised huts around the refugee camp would have proved nearly
impossible, even with a bulldozer or a couple tanks.

"So you say," Steiner answered. "It all depends on what he
decides his priority is. As it is, Stamen never answered back
from the ambush on Captain Blake and the Geren woman."

"A communications error," Rhodin spoke up. He rubbed
his bruised jaw, stretching and flexing it back into shape. "It
was a dozen men, armed with rocket-propelled grenades."

"Against at least half of a Special Forces team and their vehicles," Steiner responded. "I swear, if Stamen is dead—"

"You let Soze down," Rhodin answered.

Steiner stiffened, his thick arms going taut. Rhodin wondered if he'd just invited the sad-eyed assassin to twist the
skull from his shoulders for use as a kick ball. Fists the size
and shape of hams flexed and tensed, tendons crackling as
they stretched across heavy muscle and thick bone. The Abraham's Dagger commander had watched Steiner shatter the
necks of grown men with a single punch from those brutal
hands. If Steiner was going to punch Rhodin, the Dagger
leader took consolation that he wouldn't feel death.

"You're right, Olsen," Steiner answered. He relaxed.

"The sooner we're out of this forsaken country, the better,"
Rhodin said. "But we have to cover ourselves. We have to
show the world that those who coddle the Palestinians are not
safe—anywhere."

MACK BOLAN LEANED ON TO the Land Rover's accelerator. As
the road raced past them outside the windows, Afghanistan
became a blur.

"Stone, you're going to open up Montenegro!" Mc-
Korkindale spoke up.

"Let him drive, man!" Montenegro snapped. "He's got lives to save!"

"At the cost of our—" McKorkindale began.

"Shut your fuckin' pie hole, Mack!" Jerrud yelled.

Bolan spun his head, looking at Jerrud, then realized that he was using the nickname for the A-Team medic. He returned his concentration to the road, fingers tight around the steering wheel.

Haytham had contacted him while he was stripping gear from the shattered Humvees. Even though Bolan hated looting the vehicles of fallen fellow soldiers, he was a practical man. Supplies were needed, and he said a moment of silent thanks to the three dead American soldiers who had given their all. Now, all that was left was what Uncle Sam had issued them, and he was going to make as much use as possible of what still worked.

The Land Rover went over a bump and caught some air time, soaring twenty feet and landing, tires protesting, the frame of the vehicle whining. This wasn't the safest driving he'd ever done, but without an aircraft, there was no faster way to get to Haytham's side before the attack on the Hamas men and their captives was over.

Abraham's Dagger had tracked down the Palestinians to their headquarters in Afghanistan, and were sending a third prong of their assault against the unaware enemies. Had Tera Geren and Jason Blake not been their prisoners, the Executioner wouldn't have thought twice about going to Haytham's rescue.

Then a twinge of guilt filled him as the outskirts of Chaman loomed in the distance.

Marid Haytham was a man Bolan could understand. He was a man who was dragged into a war, driven by loss and pain. Where Bolan had turned himself into a living shield to defend the innocent, Haytham had forged himself as a sword, driving down on the men he assumed were responsible for the deaths of his loved ones.

That he didn't harm bystanders was all that the Executioner needed to know about the true state of Haytham's soul. The man was tortured and made a promise to himself he'd never let another suffer as he had. The exact same vow that drove Mack Samuel Bolan to risk his life every single day.

At least three lives were worth saving, one to be given the chance for redemption. He swung the Land Rover down the quiet streets. In the distance, he saw smoke curling up from buildings on far parts of town. One he knew instantly as Captain Blake's improvised headquarters.

The other, the closer one, was where the Palestinians had been holed up.

"It's Haytham, Colonel," Jerrud spoke up, his ear pressed to the phone. "They've lost another man."

"We're closing in," Bolan said.

"He says they don't have much time."

Bolan's eyes narrowed to a squint, twisting the steering wheel around.

"Nobody does, Sergeant," he growled. "But I'm working on it!"

TERA GEREN, HER WRISTS bound tightly behind her, was back in the conscious world the moment the wall blew in. She recalled a hazy memory of being surrounded by Palestinian men arguing her fate when an explosion went off, throwing her across the room. Blake skidded to a halt, next to her, eyes wide with shock.

Marid Haytham loomed over them, cell phone pressed to

his ear, knife in one hand, the blade glimmering in the light as Hamas gunmen were firing out the hole blown in the building by a rocket-propelled grenade.

Her throat constricted for the briefest of moments, then Haytham reached behind her and she felt her wrists were suddenly free.

"What's going on?" she shouted over the din of assault rifles. Bullets chewed into the ceiling and the wall.

"Abraham's Dagger must have found us!" Haytham responded. "Now they want you in their hands, or all of us dead!"

He handed her the knife. "Get Blake loose. We're going to need all the help we can get."

"Haytham, if they spot us with guns…" Geren began.

"Shoot them back, then," Haytham growled. "It'll be no loss!"

Geren was stunned by the comment but flipped the penknife in her hand. Blake squirmed around, giving her a chance to get at his bonds.

A shadow moved into her peripheral vision. Her body, though battered and bruised, still reacted like a machine and she dived to one side as a ribbon of quicksilver flashed in the half-sunlight pouring through the damaged roof and wall.

Rolling onto her shoulder, she came up on her feet, the penknife held parallel to her index finger. Geren looked into the eyes of a balding madman, a grin splitting his face ear to ear.

"You're not even going to get a chance to hold a gun, bitch," said Amal Sariz, the man Mossad had called one of the ten most mentally unstable members of Hamas. "I'm going to cut you from scalp to toes, and you're going to enjoy every minute of it!"

THE GRENADE EXPLOSION sent Sergeant Robert Wesley diving flat on the ground, but a moment later he was up and running to the cover of the office building, M-4 SOPMOD bouncing in its shoulder sling until he got behind some heavy stonework.

Marines and Green Berets had found their cover as soon as the waves of rifle fire started. The enemy seemed to have a small supply of explosives, much less than he would have been expected, but that was a blessing as far as Wesley was concerned. He flipped on his LASH.

"Ogden, we going to get our boys up roofside in action?" he asked.

There was no response over the main frequency. He tried adjusting the volume and only ended up with an ear full of feedback that pierced his skull like a nail through plywood. He winced and yanked out his earpiece.

Bannon slid in beside Wesley like he was stealing second base, dirt kicking up behind him, some of it raised by his passing, the rest from the volcanic eruptions of bullets striking dirt at supersonic speed. The Marine scrambled to his feet, his mirrored shades long since lost, green eyes wide, red face a mass of freckles.

"You guys know how to throw a welcome party," Bannon quipped.

"Hell, you should see us when we have more warning. Usually it's strippers with big hooters jumping out of fifty-five-gallon drums," Wesley answered.

"Wow, I'll have to try that sometime," Bannon answered. He shouldered his M-4, scanning rooftops, then ducking back under cover. "No good. They've got the high ground."

"Well, their marksmanship's shit, at least," Wesley answered. "They're doing just enough to keep our heads down."

"I don't like being stuck in a defensive position," Bannon answered. "How's your communications?"

"Someone's left us with space noise, man," Wesley replied. "I'm thinking that the renegade Israelis had some pretty spiffy tech going to shut us down."

"Comm, ammo and water is what keeps a unit going, and they knocked out one third of that," Bannon said. "And given the response we threw up when the shooting started—"

"Lord knows how long the ammo's going to last," Wesley said. "Luckily, we calmed down back to training."

Wesley poked his head out, looking for an enemy to target. The Green Berets and the Marines had all calmed down from magazine-draining blasts of autofire to short, concise bursts. Special operations soldiers learned that a light tap of the trigger, putting out between one and four rounds, resulted in more hits against the enemy than trying to wrestle against the recoil of a rifle on full-auto. Hits were what counted, and that was what made the odds more even, marksmanship and proper cover proving to be an effective way to increase the effectiveness of a unit.

Bannon yanked Wesley back behind cover as bullets sprayed the stone pillar that sheltered them. Wesley realized that the Taliban soldiers were making a textbook example of how even expert use of cover was enough to make the odds between professional soldiers and bullying thugs a draw.

"As much as I appreciate you being bait, I'd prefer to keep you on the live side of this battle," Bannon said.

"Thanks," Wesley answered. "Listen, could you cover me? We have a rooftop hide where I can get a better view of all the bad guys hemming us in."

"And maybe get to take some potshots at them too?" Bannon asked.

"Sniper's roost. Sharpshooter's heaven," Wesley promised.

"Hickcock! Plaster! Get your asses over here!" Bannon shouted, pointing to two Marines.

Wesley swung out, bringing his M-4 to his shoulder, sweeping one rooftop on full-auto, providing cover fire. Bannon's rifle barked out a similar rock-and-roll tune as the two Marines he summoned dashed wildly from their respective hiding places to his side. The two men made cover.

"These two girls happen to be the best snipers in my unit," Bannon explained as the Taliban mercenaries returned fire, bullets bouncing off stone, earth and vehicles. The racket was horrible. A quick glance told Wesley that no more than the four men he'd seen wounded in the initial volley were still out there, being cared for by fellow soldiers who held their ground, refusing to leave a buddy behind. It made the Green Beret's heart swell with pride.

They might be outgunned, outmanned and surrounded, but there was courage in this little office compound today, and the men wouldn't break, not for anything.

"All right. Hickcock and Plaster?" Wesley asked. "We now have to run to that door. Think you can make it and not get shot?"

Hickcock, a tall, lanky man with thick, curly black hair and dark, ruddy skin, looked at the gauntlet they had to run. "Well, unless it's like in a sack race, and I got Plaster here slowin' me down, I reckon I can make it. You're going to have to toss Plaster though. He don't run nowhere quick as me."

Plaster, a spread hand taller than five feet by Wesley's figuring, wrinkled his nose. "You could walk the distance and not get your narrow ass hit. Don't mind this moron. He needs to wear a straw to cast a shadow."

"Enough grab assing. Get up to the roof and start shooting, before they start getting lucky again!" Bannon ordered.

Wesley charged, boots digging into the dirt.

Almost immediately, enemy gunfire was dogging at his heels.

THE LOOK ON JERRUD'S FACE told the whole story to the Executioner as he swiftly tore himself out of his tan BDUs and pulled down the sleeves of the skintight black combat blacksuit.

"Colonel!" Jerrud began.

"You're staying here with Montenegro and McKorkindale," Bolan ordered. "Whether you do it with or without a broken jaw, make your decision now, so I can get to Blake and Rosenberg that much faster."

Jerrud sputtered for a moment, giving the Executioner an opportunity to throw on his load-bearing harness and the holsters for the Desert Eagle and the Uzi pistol. Full magazines were stuffed into each weapon, spare reloads tucked into appropriate pouches all along his harness. He slapped some black greasepaint into his palms and rubbed it across his face, taking on the appearance of a blackened mask, his grim features distinguished only by the startling ice blue of his eyes freezing Jerrud in place.

"I'll stay with the Land Rover, sir," Jerrud answered.

"Good," Bolan replied. He grabbed the head weapon he knew he was going to need for this fight, an M-4 SOPMOD with a grenade launcher attachment. It was smaller than the M-16/M-203 he usually took with him, but it still fired a 40 mm grenade with earthshaking power, and out of the shorter barrel of the M-4, the 5.56 mm bullets it spat still had man-stopping force at close quarters.

The three Green Berets looked at him slack-jawed, eyes wide with wonder. Bolan didn't blame them. He had transformed from a relatively normal looking man to what some people called an ultimate fighting machine. He didn't take any egotistical pride in such a statement, but he did appreciate the psychological effect it had. Over six feet of solid black, a human shadow bristling with handguns, knives, grenades, rifles and spare ammunition, long powerful arms and legs wrapped in muscle hugging black material that at once allowed his limbs full agility while protecting his skin and keeping him from snagging while he plunged through the battlefield in combat. He was a shadow that had stepped out of the darkness, a slice of night now visible in full daylight. Stealth wasn't the Executioner's goal, not in this instance. He wanted impact, and the impression he got from the faces of the Special Forces soldiers conveyed every ounce of the power he carried with him.

"Who are you, Colonel?" McKorkindale asked.

"That's the baddest mother ever to walk the Earth," Montenegro spoke up.

Bolan simply shook his head. In a flicker of movement, he whirled and was off, racing toward the group of gunmen who were hemming in the Palestinians.

With the clatter of assault rifle fire, it wasn't difficult for the Executioner to pin down the location of the Taliban gunmen. His eyes swept their positions, marked by muzzle-flashes and blurring figures fleeing and ducking return fire from the Hamas defenders. Their attention was fixated on the Palestinians' headquarters, a two-story apartment building that had seen better days even before an RPG-7 shell planted its 84 mm warhead into the ancient stone, sheering off a corner of the roof large enough to drive a Cadillac through.

Bolan sighted a couple of gunners racing toward the front of the building, their aim to penetrate the building and begin clearing it out from the inside while the defenders were occupied on protecting their perimeter. He cut them off in midrun, going for solid intimidation right off the bat. A 40 mm HE grenade popped from the fat barrel under his rifle, spiraling through the air to strike one of the gunmen. The impact fuse had enough time and distance to detonate, and when it struck human flesh, it went off.

Six ounces of high explosive shook the battlefield with the thundering announcement that the Executioner had arrived.

Gunfire halted completely, dozens of eyes stared at the black wraith who had entered the war grounds, minds struggling to cope with the sudden shock. A mouth opened in alarm, and Bolan triggered his rifle, putting a burst through the man's face, all but smashing his skull from his shoulders.

"Introductions are over," Bolan whispered to himself, raking the ranks of the Taliban mercenaries as they dived for cover, their rifles spitting a hailstorm of firepower at him. He'd won a few seconds of unresisted combat.

Now it was time to earn the rest of his victory.

14

The explosion distracted Sariz, but not Tera Geren. Not when she had one of the most dangerous men in the Middle East facing her down. Hesitation was tantamount to suicide, and fighting fair would only result in her being carved up like sandwich meat. With a half step, she lunged, tackling Sariz headfirst, raking him with the penknife.

The blade sought flesh and found it, slicing through Sariz's shirt and pants, opening a cut that was a foot long, but only a half-inch deep. It was enough to jar Sariz from his confusion, however, and he slammed his forearm against the side of Geren's head, lights flashing on and off behind her eyes from the jarring impact. The tough little Israeli went with the force of the blow, letting it redirect her. If she'd resisted the blow, she was certain it could have broken her neck. Instead, she rolled onto her back, landing five feet away from the Palestinian madman, his knife slicing at empty air.

Geren twisted her legs underneath her, spinning to her feet and allowing herself an uncontrolled stumble backward, letting gravity and her own wobbly legs make her a nearly impossible target. Just inches separated her from the shimmering afterimage of the Hamas killer's knife sweeping in an arc that would have laid her rib cage open at the very least, or slipped between the protective bones and into her lungs.

Using the wall for balance, she slapped it with both hands, snapped up one foot and caught Sariz in the shoulder with all of her might. There was a grunt, and she shoved off, closing distance before the murderer could bring his knife back up. She sliced down with her penknife, the little two-inch blade plunging into flesh, tearing along the biceps muscle of the man with a savage fury. With a howl of rage and surprise, he jerked back. Geren was about to press her advantage when Sariz pivoted on one foot, bringing his heel up and into her kidney, tossing her aside.

The Israeli fighter felt the knife disappear from her fingers at the same time her breath evacuated her lungs. Pain burned like an inferno up and down her torso. Teeth gritted, she forced herself to all fours, then spotted something out of the corner of her eye. With a hard push, the fireball launched herself backward, Sariz missed kicking where her ribs had been only moments before.

Wild, hate-filled eyes swiveled to lock on to her as she leaned back on her haunches.

"You missed," Geren snarled, bile bubbling in her throat and making her want to choke. Instead, she straightened her legs, leaping to her feet, fingers extending like claws and digging at her attacker's face. "My turn, fuckhole!" she shouted.

A punch swung into her back, thumping like a bass drumbeat and reverberating through her body, but Geren didn't let go. Instead, her blunt-nailed fingers sank into the soft flesh of the Palestinian's cheeks, skin beginning to tear at her death grip on his face. Blood spurted from the wounds, the force of her crush squeezing the viscous fluid like the juice of some unholy fruit. Some of it sprayed all over her face, red droplets matching the freckles on her cheeks.

Blinded with his own blood, Sariz flailed away. Without

leverage, and with Geren on his chest, arched against him at the limits of his reach, his blows peppered her back and sides. She ached, pain radiating from every new impact, but the fists weren't able to do the kind of murderous damage they would have if the Palestinian was on his feet, able to put his weight into each hammering strike.

Instead, Tera wrenched her hands around and plunged both of her thumbs into his eyes. A shriek of agony split the apartment building, slicing through the sound of gunfire.

Pulling her gore-smeared hands from the wreckage of his face, she reached down and dug into his belt for the pistol. She looked up and was surprised to see none of the Palestinians seemed to give a damn about the death struggle going on among them. She pressed the pistol into the ruined man's mouth, his hands preoccupied with trying to scrape the remnants of his features back together.

A single pull of the trigger, and it was over. Geren's heart hammered in her chest as she looked at the destruction she'd wrought. Queasiness cut through her, and she recoiled from the horror she'd created.

By now, Blake had pulled himself half-free and was reaching for the penknife that had been knocked free during the course of the battle. Haytham ran from a window and picked up the blade to help out Blake.

"He attacked me," Geren explained.

"I know. It doesn't matter now," Haytham told her. "We have to get moving. Colonel Stone has arrived."

"Colonel Stone?" Blake asked.

"He was the only one I could reach," Haytham explained. "He's fighting our attackers."

"With how many men?" Blake asked, glancing out the window. His face went pale for a moment, and Haytham dragged him back out of sight, bullets tearing into the wall where he'd been moments ago.

"How many?" Geren asked.

"He...was alone," Blake said breathlessly.

Haytham nodded. "That man would fight alone, unarmed and naked to protect those who needed him. And you had cause to doubt him?"

Geren smiled through the pain of a thousand bruises and maybe a broken bone. "I never doubted him."

THE EXECUTIONER DROPPED his doubts behind him like empty ballast, anything that slowed his combat mind spilling along with the empty brass from his hammering assault rifle. There was no sign, yet, of any of the soldiers from Abraham's Dagger, but that didn't make him feel any better. Just because an enemy soldier wasn't visible on a battlefield didn't mean he wasn't out there. Bolan had won most of his fights because he wasn't a visible target, able to strike first and fast from the shadows and fade away again.

Not this time. He had to fight to protect an ambushed set of defenders, and the Executioner knew the best way to draw the fire away from a surrounded firebase was to leave big footprints on the back of the attackers. He didn't count how many he'd chopped down with the slashing bursts from his rifle, but between his attacks, and the sniping from the hemmed in Palestinians, the assault was breaking up nicely.

Bolan took cover behind an old Yugo, feeding a fresh 40 mm shell into the grenade launcher. Just because the attack was breaking up didn't mean that he wasn't still under attack. Slugs peppered the frame of the car, punching through sheet metal, making the Executioner glad he had the full length of the car to protect him. Reloaded, he swung around the left front fender and pumped off the explosive charge at a clot of dug-in gunmen. The window front that they were fighting behind suddenly became a volcano of black smoke and charred body parts.

Bolan let the mostly empty rifle drop on its sling, drawing his Desert Eagle as an instant reload. A Taliban mercenary lunged from cover, but was thrown immediately back as a hole smashed through the center of his chest by a booming 240-grain hollowpoint round.

Bolan crouched for cover, then made a hand gesture to one of the Palestinian gunmen up high. The man caught the movement, and for a moment Bolan wasn't sure if the Hamas man was going to pull the trigger on him or help him out. The Executioner pointed ahead toward the battle-shocked street. Smoldering corpses lay askew amid chunks of rubble.

The Palestinian jerked out of sight, bullets hammering the area around the hole he'd poked out of. Bolan reacted instantly, leveling the Desert Eagle at two men with rifles who were now visible to him, partially obscured by a chest high wall. Only their heads and rifles were visible, and they were easily twenty yards away, but the powerful Magnum pistol had easily three times that range, and the accuracy to hit a target the size of a melon. He triggered the big .44 once, twice, a third time and watched two nearly decapitated terrorists tumble lifelessly, no longer threatening the Palestinian who was giving him his bird's-eye view.

The man popped out and gave the soldier a thumbs-up. Bolan spotted a bloodied bandage on his arm, and the Executioner remembered the story that Jerrud had given him. This had to have been Haytham's partner in rescuing Blake and Tera, the one hit by the overzealous idiot's hail of bullets. He gave a quick point, then ducked back behind cover.

The Executioner turned and looked for the target the Palestinian had indicated. It was like having a bird dog, Bolan momentarily mused. Except in this case, the pointer was risking his life because the pheasants didn't take flight; they took aim with rifles that spat out death at the rate of 600 rounds per minute. He caught a flash of movement and hit the ground, flat on his chest, bullets sizzling over his head. The Desert Eagle roared until it was empty and Bolan rolled hard, his left hand plucking the Uzi pistol from the shoulder holster. With a squeeze of the trigger, he was back in action, hammering the enemy gunman with a salvo of 9 mm slugs that finally stopped the two-way bulletfest.

His arm felt slick, hot and wet, and he knew that his blood was soaking through the bandage. Bolan looked away from the injury, scanning for sources of new pain.

That's when a pair of hands shot out of a doorway, grabbing him around the head and neck, pulling him back into the depths of a building. Bolan's feet kicked hard, trying to apply the brakes, his chin tucking down into his chest to keep a pair of hands or a wire from wrapping around his throat with choking force. Instead, one fist broke its grasp on him and slammed down onto his chest like a hammer, the thump making the soldier gag as breath and bile were forced up into his mouth.

Rather than concentrate on the effects of the attack, the Executioner responded to it, both hands stabbing upward, fingers clawing at exposed ears and grabbing them in a death grip. There was a snarling growl of pain as the man tried to shake his head free, but the big soldier pulled his hands down hard. Flesh ripped.

Bolan bent himself in two, bringing his ankles on either side of his enemy's neck. Pulling all of his weight back down, he rolled the guy forward and over him. In the moment that he'd caught the man in a headlock, the soldier saw that the assailant wasn't a local Taliban mercenary. He had to have been one of Abraham's Dagger.

He had memorized the file photos Tera showed him. The name Stamen crossed the Executioner's computer-like mind, but he wasn't going to be using that name much longer. Stamen whirled like a savage beast, trying to get his bearings when Bolan hammered down on him. The jolt of his fist slamming into the side of the Israeli's neck made his injured bicep spike in agony again. Blood flowed more freely through his bandages, but the assassin halted for a heartbeat.

Bolan pressed his advantage, bringing his knee up into the man's gut before wrapping his hand around the side of Stamen's head. With a savage lurch, he crashed skull bone into unresisting brick, blood and gray matter spurting from the impact point.

"Still there?" Bolan asked.

Stamen blinked his eyes, his lips trying to form words.

"Wrong answer," Bolan told him, driving his broken skull into the brick wall twice, each time increasing the size of the crimson splatter stain on the rough stone.

Stamen slid down the wall, eyes staring blankly up at his executioner.

Bolan saw people running for him and swung his rifle from its sling toward them, only to see Haytham, Blake and Tera. Bolan raised the muzzle and loaded a fresh magazine into place.

"What kept you?" Geren asked.

"Traffic," Bolan replied. "Are you three okay?"

"We're standing," Blake said. From the way his knees wobbled, the breath coming in ragged bursts from his mouth, he was a long way from convincing Bolan of the truth of that. "You came all this way to turn yourself in?"

"No," Bolan said, jacking a fresh round into his rifle's breech.

"Good. I'm too fucking tired to arrest you anyway," Blake panted.

"Haytham, what kind of transportation do you have?" Bolan asked.

More Palestinians came out into the street, all of them regarding the Executioner and his companions with a level of distrust. He turned toward them, eyes narrowing.

"Oh, by the way, there were two opinions about how to deal with me," Geren spoke up.

"Let me guess…you killed one of them," Bolan said, looking at her red hands.

"Their leader," Haytham explained. "But he tried to kill her first."

Bolan cut through his circle of companions, stopping between them and the Palestinians.

"I just risked my life to help you against the Israelis and their hired killers," Bolan said. "And I need your help."

The Hamas men looked at him. Bolan, covered in blood, black greasepaint, midnight dark blacksuit, was an imposing sight standing before them. He unkinked his shoulders, cold blue eyes never blinking as he glared at them. "I am interested in finding the men who slaughtered innocent Palestinian women and children in the name of defending their country. Such cowards deserve to be hunted down and exterminated. You're here on that mission, and that makes you a righteous ally in my book. We can work as a team, or we can be enemies. I don't have time to make this choice into a long debate."

The Palestinians quickly began whispering to one another.

"Are you with me?" Bolan repeated.

"We are," Sellil spoke up. "Where can we get justice, Colonel?"

"Follow me," the Executioner responded. "It's your turn to be the Marines."

WITH HICKCOCK AND PLASTER hot on his heels, Wesley was charging across the gauntlet of Taliban gunfire. Rifles were chewing and spitting out thunderous volleys of death. The three racing Americans kept their legs pumping. For all the joking previously about Plaster's slowness and Hickcock's skinniness, the two men were taking this race against flying murder deadly serious. All that mattered now was crossing the nine, eight, seven yards to the door.

Hickcock tripped, his long spindly arms flailing for air, but Plaster's thick, short arm reached out, hooked the tall Marine's arm and yanked him closer to him, cradling him like he was a football. Wesley threw his hand back and grabbed Hickcock's other forearm and continued on, two racing sets of feet dragging the squirming man along. It took all of a heartbeat for them to cross two more yards, bullets still hammering their footsteps.

Wesley didn't bother opening the glass doors. Unleathering his 9 mm Beretta and emptying the clip as he approached, he shattered the glass and left it a weakened mass of spider-webbed glazing. He tucked his head down, put one polycarbonate-shelled elbow pad up and hit the weakened barrier. For a moment, he stopped, the fractured pane holding against his weight, but Plaster and Hickcock both threw themselves against his back. All three of them tumbled through, sending a cascade of broken, diamondlike cubes skittering across the floor in front of them.

"Everyone alive?" Wesley asked.

"Fuckin' A," Plaster muttered.

Hickcock shrugged. "Weren't nothin' we didn't do in basic."

Wesley grinned at Marine modesty at its finest, then got to his feet, leading the way up the stairs. As they climbed, he slapped a fresh magazine into his Beretta, reholstered it and transitioned to the M-4 SOPMOD. The pistol itself was a good weapon, but it wouldn't have the kind of reach and punch to take out enemy riflemen on distant rooftops, especially if they were behind any kind of cover. With ground-eating strides, he reached the rooftop and kicked open the door.

A rain of steel-cored slugs swept through the doorway and Wesley dropped to the ground. Hickcock and Plaster luckily were half a flight lower. All three soldiers took cover against the steps as enemy bullets crashed through the rooftop access.

"Too much firepower up there!" Wesley said to the others. "We can't do a damn thing!"

Plaster shook his head. "We made that run for nothing?" A slab of stone dropped just in front of the stocky little Marine's face and he recoiled from it.

Hickcock calmly wiped dust from his goggles and looked around. "This place is too urban, too many civilians in the area for us to call in Marine air support."

"Any kind of air support," Wesley muttered. He felt the cell phone that Stone had given him begin to vibrate and pulled it out. "Colonel Stone?"

"It's Blake," came a familiar voice. "Stone's busy."

"Sir," Wesley began. "I can explain—"

"Can the explanations. We're at war. We'll just call it a breakdown in communications," Blake said. "Speaking of communications breakdown, someone's knocked out traditional radio broadcast in the area. We're using cell phones and that makes us assume that the enemy's using phones too."

"I wish I knew where they were jamming from, because

then we could start getting word out that we need evacuation or support," Wesley answered.

"Someone's on his way to help you out with that," Blake said.

"I'll believe it when I see it, sir!" Wesley said.

"I'm seeing it, and I'm still not believing it," Blake answered.

MACK BOLAN KNEW HE HAD only one chance to get to high enough ground to give the pinned down Marines and Green Berets at Chaman some breathing room. He rolled the Land Rover as close as he could to the tallest building in the district. Shell casings bounced off the roof of the vehicle and the sidewalk around him, letting the soldier know that he was going to need to do some fast cleanup work the moment he hit the rooftop. He did one last check of the Desert Eagle and the Uzi pistol, then cinched his M-4 tight against his back and brought the big BCB International 7080 Grapnel launcher to his shoulder.

Tera Geren looked at him, holding the loops of grapnel coil, looking back toward their wheels. "You could just take the stairs," she said.

"And be too tired to fight when I get up there? Or have no one left to fight for?" Bolan asked. He nodded to the winch that was jury-rigged tightly to the front fender of the Land Rover. The lashings that bound the winch to the vehicle had been stripped off a crippled Humvee, and he hoped it would be enough to take what he had in mind. Half of the spool of launcher rope was spilled on the ground, only the very end hooked to a rappelling harness around his hips—another prize from the Green Beret's wreckage. The other end of the line was being hooked up to the winch by Haytham.

"When the hook gets up there, it's going to attract a lot of attention anyway," Haytham said.

"I'll take my chances," Bolan said. "Clear the tube."

Geren handed him the grapnel hook and stepped back. Bolan dropped the warhead into the muzzle of the mortar. Pneumatic pressure launched the lightweight carbon-fiber hook at tremendous velocity, sailing it up and over the edge of the roof. He tossed the big launcher to Geren and grabbed the cord as it snapped like a whip against his palms.

"C'mon," he gritted to the grapnel, willing it to snag on the rooftop. It wasn't the easiest shot in the world. The line yanked taut against him, and Bolan winced as the straps cut into him, then watched the cord grow slack as the hook was dragged back down by gravity.

The rope stopped dropping in loops, and Bolan's sharp blue eyes locked on the grapnel hook, hanging on the edge of the rooftop. "Haytham!"

The winch yanked hard and Bolan gripped the rope with one hand, his long legs reaching in looping steps to keep his balance as he was pulled up the side of the building. He knew that if his feet slipped out from under him, he'd be dragged up the concrete like cheese across the face of a grater. Or his rope harness could snap or the hook could be dislodged by his weight or the effort of a terrorist on the roof, and he'd fall to the ground, either to die or end up with a shattered spine.

Dying is not an option, he told himself. He'd faced death too many times to fear its chilling breath. Dying was not the Executioner's plan, not when there were still people who needed him. Shirking his own safety to do what needed to be done was his duty to humankind as a whole.

Bolan's right foot slipped, and suddenly he was parallel to the wall, his knees hitting stone. Electric jolts of pain shot up his thighs and down his shins, and he bounced away from the building, the rope creaking as his weight shifted crazily. He knew that if he bounced again off the side of the building, he'd start losing control, and the winch, the grapnel hook, or both would become unsettled and unbalanced by his whirling form. Splaying his legs, he hit the wall again, and flexing his limbs, cushioning the shock and absorbing his momentum. His feet came a couple of inches back off the wall, but he stretched to keep the soles of his boots up against the rough surface.

He returned his attention to the rooftop ahead when a solitary figure leaned over the ledge, rifle pointing down. The man cried out, and Bolan's hand dropped to the Desert Eagle in its holster. But he knew it was going to be too late.

15

Heavy-caliber rifle bullets tore past. Trapped on the side of a building, being dragged up by a rope, he had no options to duck, dodge or escape. As fast as he was on the draw, there was no way for him to pull his pistol and punch a hole through the chest of the man trying to kill him.

The Executioner waited what seemed like an eternity for the terrorist's aim to improve, when he realized that there was no muzzle-flash issuing from the man's weapon. With a jerk, the man seized up, his AK falling from lifeless fingers, the stock bouncing off Bolan's injured arm, making him choke back a cry of pain. He glanced down to see Geren and Haytham, rifles raised toward the heavens, ready to gun down any man who aimed at Bolan.

He showed the pair a thumbs-up, and kept going, keeping his balance, carefully crawling up the side of the building like some gigantic spider. Finally, after what felt like hours, though his watch only read three and a half minutes, he was at the top ledge of the building. He clamped one hand over the ledge and wrapped his other around the grip frame of his Uzi pistol. His shooting arm had taken beating after beating over the past few days, and he wasn't going to trust that arm to hold his weight seventy feet above the ground, although he could still shoot and punch with relative ease.

The muscles in his left arm swelled, and his legs pushed off hard. With a surging leap, he was on the rooftop, Uzi up and tracking targets.

The Taliban gunmen were surprised by the sudden appearance of over six feet of solid black muscle and steel weaponry. One rifleman spun and triggered his weapon, the stream of gunfire tracking too slowly to catch up with the approaching Executioner, who triggered his own Uzi only after lining up the front sight post, making sure that the weapon was on-target. Where the terrorist was only wasting ammunition, Bolan was wasting him with a precision burst of 9 mm slugs.

Panic set in as the riflemen were torn between fleeing for their lives and opening up with their weapons. It looked to Bolan, for all the world, like a Keystone Kops episode, with four men slamming into one another in a tangle of limbs. One gunman accidentally triggered his autoweapon into the groin of another, dropping him in a pile at the feet of the three others who still struggled, unbalanced and confused.

That confusion turned out to be fatal as Bolan swept them with an extended burst, burning off half the magazine. The hot slugs punched through flesh, causing the gunners to cry out, wither and die. The Executioner sidestepped the jumble of terrorists. Stuffing the Uzi back in its harness, he pulled the M-4 from its sling on his back. He came to a halt, kneeling before a three-foot segment of wall that framed the rooftop. He'd never properly sighted in the scoped carbine, and knew that whoever had shot the weapon before him would have had a different hand-eye coordination. That would put shots off to such a degree that he could miss enemy gunmen at even fifty yards away.

The Executioner decided to test points of impact with a close up shot, lining up the crosshairs on the upper chest of a gunman some twenty yards distant. The Taliban shooter suddenly turned. The amplification of the M-4's scope allowed Bolan to see his target's eyes widen with horror. Bolan stroked the trigger and saw the bullet impact the man's face above his right eyebrow, instead of his left cheekbone where the crosshairs rested.

Having gotten his range, he swung toward another of the rooftop gunmen. Three more shooters had the sentences of their lives punctuated by Executioner marksmanship before the raining hail of death on the U.S. Special Forces compound stopped.

From his sniping post, Bolan spotted uncertainty and fear spreading like shock waves among the Taliban fighters. He counted nine dead. That left over thirty shooters still unaccounted for across the various rooftops.

Bolan felt his phone vibrate on his hip as he tucked down behind the wall.

"It's Blake. Wesley told me that someone's jamming communications. Can you see anything?" The Special Forces captain was all work, no bull on the phone. Bolan appreciated that in the man. They could work together after all.

"I was counting heads, not antennas," Bolan responded. "I'll take a look."

"You do that, but give my boy and those two Marines some cover fire so they can get to their position," Blake said. It sounded like an order, but Bolan didn't mind.

He saw one of the enemy riflemen shouting into his cell phone. A tinny voice echoed upward from the other side of the pile of bodies he'd created with a slash of Uzi fire moments before. Bolan scrambled over to the dead man's phone, listening to a breathless rambling in Arabic, almost too fast for him to understand. He got the gist of it, though. The Taliban gunmen were trying to coordinate and figure out why two rooftops full of snipers had suddenly stopped shooting.

Bolan lifted his rifle again and took snap-aim at the man calling into the phone, trying to coordinate the enemy efforts. He didn't have the kind of electronics gear needed to blind the enemy, so he'd have to do it the old-fashioned way, one bullet at a time.

The 5.56 mm slug struck the phone man's hand. In shock and pain he stumbled and fell over the ledge to the ground. Faces contorted in rage and shock, stunned by the sudden death of their leader.

The gunners looked frantically for the source of the shot. The Executioner decided to give them some clues, flicking the selector switch on the M-4 and hammering off 2- and 3-round bursts. Supersonic bullets punched through rib cages, tearing apart lungs and heart muscle after shredding themselves on the heavy curved rib bones they shattered. He ducked back down as half the city's rooftops seemed to come alive with the lightning flash and snap-crackle of dozens of AK-47s hammering all at once. Brick was pulverized and Bolan crawled, scrambling toward the front corner of the roof.

Any moment, the enemy would return its attention to the easier targets down below, and all that Bolan had risked would have been for naught. He popped up and looked for targets, specifically whoever was jamming the radio transmitter.

He spotted a group of gunmen, one of whom was separated from the rest and sitting out the fight. He tilted the muzzle to allow for bullet drop from the short-barrel assault carbine, and ripped off a burst that was dead on. The dying man tumbled backward, and Bolan had the range thanks to the scope and where his bullets hit the target. Shifting his grip on the weapon, he wrapped his hand around the rifle's magazine, index finger looping through the trigger guard of the grenade launcher. He froze as a face appeared in a window just under the rooftop. Bolan focused the sights on the opening. A frightened child's face appeared for a moment before hands pulled it out of sight.

High explosives and innocent bystanders, even with the protection of a roof, were not a mixture the Executioner was willing to stir together. He forgot about taking out the jammer with the 40 mm and rested the crosshairs on the compact packet of electronics, once more adjusting for gravity and wind resistance. A pull of the trigger caused sparks and chunks of the transmitter to fly off. A second, more sustained blast kicked the unit along like a soccer ball, tumbling it toward the edge of the roof, entire sections flying apart, circuit boards scattering to the wind.

He plugged in his earphone and soon the tactical net was alive with voices. Blake was barking orders as he huffed and puffed his way up the stairs. Bolan smiled and watched as the combined force of Marines and Green Berets, scattered across the compound and under heavy fire, started to communicate. He glanced across to Wesley, who shot Bolan a big thumbs-up as he raced toward the sniper's hide.

"Wesley, keep down!" Bolan called.

An Arab gunman swung his rifle around, focusing on the new intruders at rooftop level, visible and vulnerable. Bolan could see Wesley take a half step, bringing up his own rifle. The Executioner tried to track the line of sight that the Special Forces trooper was making. The Taliban shooter that Wesley aimed at bent in two, as if struck in the stomach with an ax handle. The gunman flopped back lifelessly, his intestines pouring out of a pie-pan-sized hole in his abdomen.

Bolan's gut tightened, not at the carnage, but at a dread

feeling. He spun back and saw a gaunt scarecrow of a Marine hauling Wesley into the rooftop sniper's hide, bullets smashing the roof around the two men. The Executioner flicked the M-4's muzzle and fired off a burst toward the shooters closest to Wesley. The magazine ran dry after ten rounds.

It was enough to draw enemy fire toward him and away from the vulnerable Americans, and Bolan ducked down, feeding a fresh magazine into his carbine as he listened to bullets pop like hailstones against the other side of the wall he was nestled against. Wesley was down, and there was no telling how badly he was wounded. Even the combat load-bearing vests they wore didn't have enough trauma protection to completely stop a steel-cored, armor-piercing 7.62 mm round. A sustained burst would turn even the best armored soldier into so much ground chuck.

With an aching heart, Bolan pushed aside thoughts of Wesley, returning to the task of helping break the back of the Taliban assault on the Chaman command post.

Lives had to be saved.

CAPTAIN JASON BLAKE burst out onto the rooftop, McKorkindale, Jerrud, Sellid and Fasood in tow. He saw Stone shooting from his rooftop, raining accurate fire on the Taliban shooters as fast as he could track them. He waved out the group he was with, looking for anybody still capable of fighting on top of this building, M-4 sweeping for threats.

"Clear!" Jerrud announced over his radio.

He looked over to Fasood, who raised his hand and made a sweeping cut horizontally. He shook his head to reinforce the point.

This rooftop was home to his group, and a bunch of dead bodies.

Blake looked over to the compound and saw a mess. Craters from where RPGs had slammed into the ground smoked, thick black columns spiraling skyward. Not a single pane of glass was intact. One wall of the entrance was chewed to pieces by what had to have been a solid battering ram. He couldn't conceive of simple automatic rifle fire doing that much damage to concrete, at least until he looked up and saw the chewed apart section on the roof that Stone was working from.

"Ogden, what's the sitrep down there?" Blake asked.

"I've got two of ours wounded, one serious. We also ended up with seven injured and one dead Marine," Ogden answered. "We could have a couple more dead if we don't get medevacs in here."

"How far out are they?" Blake asked.

"Just got on the horn with them now. We can count on ten, fifteen minutes, but that might not be soon enough," Ogden answered.

Blake sighed. "You've got Marines up there with our people?"

"They're the only ones on their feet," Ogden said.

Blake watched as the two Marines started their methodical sweep of the rooftops, rifles cracking, one shot one kill. Every Marine was a rifleman, and the lowest level of skill allowable for each member of the Corps was to be a marksman. While the Palestinians kicked up a lot of brass with little effect, and his Green Berets were making the enemy sweat, the two sharpshooters were knocking down a man with each pull of the trigger.

Colonel Stone was doing more of the same. Only Jerrud, his own A-team's sniper specialist seemed to be keeping pace with the other three men.

It felt anticlimactic at this point, terrorists dropping as a coordinated effort hit the rooftops. More Marines and Green Berets moved down below. Vehicles that could operate were starting up. He keyed his radio.

"I want status reports, all channels," Blake called in.

"This is Captain Kitchner, USMC," an unfamiliar voice broke in. "Sorry we showed up too late for your trip this morning."

"Well, I'm glad you guys still had something interesting to do," Blake said. He turned to McKorkindale and waved him on. "We're going to need all of our medics it looks like."

"Yeah. My boys Hickcock and Plaster are trying to keep your man Wesley stable," Kitchner answered. "You might want to get down here."

Blake looked around the battle scene. The gunfire had faded, and he glanced to Colonel Stone, who was already hooking himself to the climbing rope and rappelling down from the roof. "All right, it's clear. Everyone to the compound."

"And how do we know you're not going to try to drag us in?" Sellid asked.

Blake's eyes narrowed. "We're operating under a flag of truce. We have a mutual enemy."

Sellid nodded.

"Colonel Stone, are you on the net?" Blake asked.

"Yeah. What kind of transportation are we getting in here?" the man in black asked.

"We at least have medevacs and their escorts," Blake returned. "What do you need?"

"Something fast," Mack Bolan said, grunting as his feet struck the ground. "And if you can arrange an airstrike on a convoy of trucks heading toward the Makaki refugee camp and hospital—"

"Makaki?" Blake asked. "There are thousands of people

there. Kitchner, do you think Marine aviation can send up some airpower to knock out the trucks?"

"It'd be like shootin' fish in a barrel, unless the convoy got too close to civilians," Kitchner said. "Colonel Stone, you said you needed fast transportation? We have a couple Hueys coming in for medevac."

"They're supposed to get your wounded to treatment."

"They have SuperCobra gunship escorts—four of them—considering the fight we just had," Kitchner replied.

"It's seventy-five miles to the refugee camp, and Abraham's Dagger has at least a thirty-minute head start on us. If we can get the Cobras to take a couple of us—"

"Contacting the incoming escorts," Kitchner stated. "Not going to guarantee that you'll get more than two of them to take you to Makaki. Marine pilots don't like leaving their gunners or their slicks behind."

"One would be enough, and two would be ideal," Bolan said.

Breathless moments were passing, and Blake spent them racing down the stairs, exiting the building at ground level and returning to his HQ. He couldn't help but feel self-recrimination at the sight of injured men on the ground. One body was overlaid with a tarpaulin, never to rise again. The dull self-recrimination became a knife of guilt in his chest.

The tall shape of Colonel Stone appeared at his side as Marines brought down another form on an improvised stretcher.

It was Wesley, and his eyes stared glassily. The captain felt his own face tighten in sympathy to the pained mask Wesley wore.

"Colonel?" Wesley whispered. Blake could see where the short, puglike Marine was pressing a wound dressing to the man's stomach, the gauze soaked through. Around his neck was another hasty wrapping, which was less bloody. Neither Marine's face held much hope.

The tall warrior in black leaned over him. "I'm here. What was the big idea moving around and shooting people on that roof?"

Wesley chuckled, then coughed. "That's what I went up there for in the first place. There were just a few too many targets for these two jarheads to handle."

"We could have handled it," Plaster said. "He took a second hit. He was too slow getting back under cover."

"It was just a dumb, lucky hit," the wounded man whispered.

"Just keep quiet. Medevac's on its way." Blake tried to soothe him.

"But I got a call—" Wesley said. "It was Laith Khan. He said he spotted the convoy, and it's fifteen minutes away from Makaki."

Blood burbled from his lips and he looked at Bolan squarely. "You have to get there in time, sir."

Mack Bolan took Wesley's hand and gave it a squeeze. "I'll do it."

Wesley closed his eyes.

Blake shook his head, his whole body tensing up, trying to hold back a wave of riotous anger. "I've lost too many people to these animals—"

"You won't lose any more," Bolan said. He looked up, catching sight of the helicopters coming in.

"What are you talking about?" Blake asked. "You're going to need backup at Makaki."

"And this place is going to need to be kept under control," Bolan said. "Kitchner is going to need assistance, and if we can't handle a convoy of Taliban trucks with two Cobra gunships, then your tagging along won't help. Secure this area.

Central command is counting on you, and there's probably a lot more hurt and frightened civilians who can use the humanitarian assistance."

Blake took a deep breath, letting it out in a slow shudder. "You're right, Colonel."

"I'm not going to let the bastards who did this get away," Bolan promised. "But there are just too many lives at stake to be squabbling about who can fit into the cockpit of a Cobra."

A tall man with a nose like an ax blade and a tightly trimmed Vandyke ran up. When he spoke, Blake recognized him immediately as Captain Kitchner.

"I've got two Cobras volunteering to ferry you and whoever else you need, Colonel Stone," Kitchner spoke up.

"All right," Bolan said. He looked around and realized that except for himself, Tera Geren and the Palestinians, every trained man here would be needed for emergency relief and to secure the area against any remaining Taliban thugs. "Tera, you're coming with me."

"What about me?" Haytham asked.

"We don't have enough helicopters to go around," Bolan told Haytham. "These are two-seaters."

"Yeah, well, I can ride in his lap," Geren said. "Just because you're closing in on seven feet long and have no room for your knees in a Cobra, doesn't mean I can't squish down onto Haytham's lap."

The Palestinian leader smiled, nodding in agreement with the spunky little Israeli fireball. "Colonel Stone, you promised to help me take a hand in justice. I want to be there to take the fight to the real enemy."

"We could use a third set of eyes on the ground if it comes to that," Geren added.

Bolan frowned. By the time the Cobras reached Makaki, Abraham's Dagger would have been in place for easily ten minutes. Enough time to send assassins ahead to stake out and target the last two witnesses. He checked his watch.

Time was running out.

"If you two can fit, so be it. Otherwise, you get to fight to the death to see who rides shotgun in the second Cobra," Bolan said.

The Cobras swung down to land in the office compound. Bolan raced toward the closer gunship, dread in his gut with the knowledge that he was already ten minutes too late.

16

Laith Khan looked at his watch, put his binoculars to his eyes, then checked his watch again. The phone sat silent in his pocket as Dr. Bronson tried to convince Koenig and Takeda to at least join them in the jeep. Laith glanced over to the rifle propped up in the shotgun seat, just one grab away from cutting loose on full-auto, and it still didn't seem like enough.

He remembered the trucks, and he couldn't begin to put the numbers together of how many men could be packed into the backs of them. Abraham's Dagger was nowhere in sight, though. Not yet. The road to Makaki wasn't empty, but it was tottering buses, bicycles and donkey-drawn carriages that approached, not a fleet of military transports.

He'd never felt so alone in his life.

The phone rang in his pocket.

"Colonel?" he spoke as soon as he opened the cell.

"We're on our way. Is anything happening yet?" Bolan asked him.

Laith brought the binoculars to his eyes again, scanning the road, sweeping the horizon, but came up with nothing. "No enemy traffic yet, but I can't see far. A mile and a half at best, thanks to all the tents in my way."

"Where are the doctors?"

Laith took a look over to the tent. "Debating on whether they should stand their ground or run away again, sounds like."

"Is Bronson telling them that standing their ground is suicide?" Bolan asked.

"Sometimes suicide is the painless way out," Laith answered. He kept his eyes on the road. "Mikela feels bad enough. The three of them sounded like they'd take their fate standing up."

"I was afraid of that," Bolan admitted.

"Colonel?"

"You're going to stay and fight, aren't you?"

Laith cleared his throat. "My uncle taught me about duty. He told me you understand."

"I do. Be careful. I'm only eight miles away," the Executioner said.

Laith lowered the binoculars, letting them fall on the strap around his neck, their weight striking his chest, the impact unnoticed as he reached for his rifle. "The convoy is here."

BOLAN HEARD THE WORDS come over the phone and looked at his pilot. "Lieutenant?"

There was the whirr of machinery over the helmet com link that Bolan recognized as the targeting optics of the sleek, sharklike warcraft that sliced through the sky. "We have them. Range, 3.6 miles. It'll be cutting it close with the Hydra-70s."

Bolan took the gunnery controls, looking at the Hellfire aiming monitor. "I know the range on the rocket pods. And we're in range for the missiles too."

"Minigun's locked and out of your way, Colonel," the pilot, a man named Kent, said. "I just hope—"

"Hold that hope," Bolan ordered. He lined up the crosshairs on the farthest truck in the convoy, knowing that he had to break up the attack as soon as he could. The more vehicles that got close to the Makaki camp, the more chance that the fighting would end up among the refugees.

Too many good people had died already, and the sun had only been up a couple of hours. The Executioner wasn't going to let more innocent blood spill if he could help it.

He triggered the Hellfire, watching it accelerate to its maximum velocity. On the monitor, he saw the truck growing larger, and he kept the joystick on the view of the bed. As the image grew clearer and more distinct, he saw that the truck was only sparsely filled with gunmen. The image suddenly turned to static as the Hellfire missile with its warhead detonated. On the horizon, an inverted pyramid of smoke and debris shot upward, forming a halolike cloud over the shattered truck.

"If that wasn't a kill, it sure got their attention," Kent said. He was right. On the targeting panel, Bolan could see the speeding blips of trucks suddenly accelerating, racing away from one another.

He hit the firing stud, seeing a couple of trucks racing off the road at such an angle that he could unleash a salvo of artillery rockets. The powerful explosive darts hurtled along the three and one-quarter miles between the helicopter and the convoy. The truck drivers probably didn't even know they were under the hammer until the supersonic slammers smashed into them. Two vehicles were chewed apart by detonations, the sand around them boiling with shock waves.

Three down and nine to go, according to Laith, but Bolan's instincts were on red alert. He counted only eight, and the trucks seemed like they'd let off some of their forces. He didn't believe it was because they were short of manpower. Not with the amount of men thrown at the Palestinians and American soldiers back at Chaman.

Bolan targeted another truck with a Hellfire and split it in two. He glanced over to the other SuperCobra, knowing that even if Geren or Haytham knew how to operate the gunnery controls, they wouldn't have been able to operate them in the narrow confines of the cockpit, not with both of them stuffed into one seat. The second helicopter was relegated to being a transport, at least until they got within range with their M197 20 mm cannon, which the pilots could aim with the sophisticated targeting systems in their flight helmets.

The Executioner, except for Kent behind him, was on his own.

The SuperCobra was eating distance greedily, and he popped off another trio of Hydra-70s, watching another truck disappear in a fireball, fragments of steel and flesh flying in thousands of directions. Always, he was scanning the desert around the edge of the refugee camp. He spotted them, finally. Men—at least twenty—running on foot.

They were close enough to use the helicopter's guns. Finally the second gunship could act.

The other SuperCobra dipped and accelerated toward another truck, its 20 mm cannon spitting fire now. The vehicle disappeared in a rainstorm of explosive shells, the pilot swerving and darting, bringing his cannon to bear on a second, and then a third target in the enemy convoy.

It was as if two gods had reached down smashing old, unwanted toys. Bolan held his fire as Kent cut loose with his cannon as well. There was only one target left.

It didn't matter. As fast as the truck accelerated, trying to escape, it was doomed as the 20 mm hellstorm flashed out. The result was as expected—complete destruction.

"That's not all," Bolan said before the explosion reached its climax.

"It never is," Kent answered. "Where do you need to be put down?"

"Drop me at the hospital. We have to get ahead of the Taliban terrorists," Bolan told him. "If we can, then maybe I can contain any conflict away from civilians."

Kent looked around. "I don't envy your job."

MARID HAYTHAM WAS GLAD to be back on the ground again, free to move on his own, uncramped by steel or even the pinning form of Tera Geren. He felt naked, even with the Makarov filling his fist, but when they'd crammed into the gunship together, there was no way they could fit their rifles, even the compact Uzi he carried, in with them. He looked back as the pilot of their helicopter, Wayne, gave them a wave.

"You're going to need something more than your pistols," the Marine said. He produced a weapon from his seatside. "Ever use the P-90?"

Haytham took the gun. It looked more like an advanced wood-planing device than a gun. He looked it over. "Magazine on the top. Trigger?"

"It ejects out the bottom, so it's fully ambidexterous," Wayne told him. "There's no thumb safety, and pressure on the trigger determines how many shots you fire. A light pull and you get one shot. Mash it down, and you'll be in rock-and-roll heaven. Clips hold fifty."

Haytham took a couple spare magazines and looked at the pilot. Doubt had to have been written across his face.

"I don't know you from Adam," Wayne told him. "But the man who ordered us to the rescue here, he trusts you. I'll take that as a good sign."

Haytham smiled. "Thank you, sir."

"There's another P-90 in the front," Wayne told Geren, and

she leaned in, taking it and its spare ammunition. "Good hunting," he said.

"I hope so," Geren replied. "Thanks."

The two people whirled and went to meet Bolan, who was standing by a jeep. Haytham recognized the young man with him as Laith Khan, the nephew of one of Afghanistan's most powerful *mujahideen* leaders.

"Too bad there's so many civilians around," Laith said. "Those Cobras could kick some serious ass."

"They did their job," Bolan told him. "Now it's time for us to earn our pay."

"Where are the doctors?" Haytham asked.

Bolan nodded toward the prefab hospital building. "At least the walls will do something to slow down some bullets."

"It took a lot of arm twisting to get them to go in there," Laith said. "But when you started blowing up half the desert—"

"They got the point," Geren finished.

"That's right," Laith answered. "How many do you think got through?"

"Too many," Bolan answered. He shifted his grip on his M-4.

"Tera, Marid, you two take that side," Bolan ordered. "Laith, stay by the entrance."

"And you?" Haytham asked.

The Executioner's voice was grim. "I'm going hunting."

REFUGEES LOOKED at the stranger as he strode through the camp, their eyes wide with surprise. Bolan remembered he was still wearing the midnight black greasepaint on his face and hands, and to them, he probably didn't look human.

People scattered at the sight of him, keeping their distance, which was exactly what the Executioner wanted. Anyone near him could end up catching a bullet if he encountered the remaining members of Abraham's Dagger or their Taliban strike force.

No sooner had he thought it than the devils themselves rose, en masse.

A trio of them tore around a corner from where they were waiting in ambush. Rifles chattered, but Bolan hit the ground, bullets spitting over his head. People around him were also dropping, screams of terror almost drowning out gunfire.

The Executioner put the crosshairs of his scope on the chest of one enemy gunman, pumping a 2-round burst through his rib cage that tossed him aside like trash. Bolan rolled over once, his wounded shoulder protesting as his weight crushed into it. He put another three shots into the torso of the second of the three gunmen, eliminating his menace.

Bullets chewed into the ground, advancing toward the Executioner. He was glad that the aim was low, as there was less chance for a shot to leave the immediate battleground. It also meant that the enemy gunman wasn't quite keeping up with him. Bolan swung his M-4 on the would-be murderer, slicing a 6-round burst, from shoulder to shoulder, nearly decapitating the rifleman.

The sound of autofire rattled behind Bolan, and he quickly got back to his feet. He saw Laith Khan opening fire on a pair of Taliban shooters who were charging the prefab hospital. Bolan swung his carbine around and punched a 3-round burst between the shoulder blades of one of the gunmen while the other buckled under the storm of impacts from Laith's rifle.

A line of exploding stone signaled the slash of another automatic weapon, a swarm of bullets racing for Laith. Bolan dashed forward, heart almost in his throat. He was going to see another of his allies felled in action, and he had no angle on the gunman. Laith pivoted and opened fire, then stumbled, puffs of sand flying from his chest.

The young man dropped to his knees, rifle falling from numbed hands as the Executioner raced toward the hospital.

Two more Taliban mercenaries raced out, one from Bolan's left and one from his right, looking to take advantage of the soldier while he was on the move. They hadn't counted on facing a fighting machine. As much as Mack Bolan, the man, was stricken with concern for his fellow human beings, the Executioner was a combat computer in a finely tuned body. Firing on the run, even from the hip, was a task the warrior had trained for and had done in the field a thousand times before. He knew where his rounds would hit just on pure base reflex.

Two squirts of 5.56 mm supersonic rounds, and the Arabs were dying.

Bolan exploded into the clearing around the hospital, spotting a quartet of gunmen taking cover behind a stack of water pipes. The buttstock of his carbine met his shoulder, and he took them, 2- and 3-shot bursts smacking into skulls, dead on target in the crosshairs of the scope. He felt a round glance off him, and when he looked down, he saw pouches torn from his load-bearing vest, Kevlar frayed by the passing of an enemy slug.

The Executioner didn't count how close the hit came, nor did he pay attention to the searing ache in his side where the 7.62 mm thunderbolt had been stopped by the combination of body armor and gear layered around his ribs. Gunfire rattled behind him, and he spun in reaction to it. He watched a Taliban gunner dance as Marid Haytham opened up on him. A second shooter popped into view, taking aim at the both of them, but Bolan's and Haytham's guns ripped him apart.

The Executioner looked toward Laith and saw Tera Geren

dragging him into the hospital, assisted by men and women in scrubs. Laith appeared to struggle, trying to get up and rejoin the fight, but a half dozen pairs of hands were unwilling to let the injured Afghan rejoin the conflict.

Reassured at the safety of his young companion, Bolan swung around, looking for more targets. He glanced at Haytham, who was similarly on the alert, his dark eyes wide and wild, black hair matted to his forehead.

"Take that side," Bolan told him.

The Palestinian gave a curt nod, pausing only to insert a fresh magazine into his FN P-90. Weapon fully loaded, Haytham swung around the corner. Bolan felt reassured at the Hamas fighter's professionalism in combat, and hoped that, odds willing, the Middle Eastern warrior would have a chance to change his life around.

Bolan turned to the other side of the building, rifle at the ready. His fingers brushed for a spare magazine, but they found nothing except the tender, sore area where at least one AK-47 round had hammered him. The pouches that held his spare ammunition had saved him from perforation, but had been torn free in the collision. That left the Executioner with only one carbine with an unknown amount of ammunition. He cast it aside and pulled out the Uzi pistol. A quick glance let him check that it was topped off, and he scanned for more snipers.

Almost a dozen of the enemy were already down, but the soldier didn't want to rest on any assumptions. The Taliban troop trucks seemed understaffed, and he didn't know if that was because they had unloaded half of their number for a pedestrian assault, or that they had simply wanted to spread the few numbers they had across a greater area by using more vehicles. Either way, one truck came up missing from the convoy, and that could have easily held two dozen men on its own.

And Bolan still hadn't seen any more members of Abraham's Dagger, and three of them were unaccounted for.

Every instinct screamed that they were still out there.

Three Taliban gunmen burst out of an alley from the shantytowns, and Bolan brought up his Uzi to meet them. They were already coming under fire, sharp rifle cracks resounding as slugs sliced into the gunmen from behind. One of the Arab riflemen spun. He screamed and leveled his AK-47 at whoever shot at his companions, but the Executioner cut him off at the waist with a sizzling swarm of 9 mm hornets that tore open the gunner's belly. The thug glanced toward Bolan, eyes stricken with some unexplained betrayal, mouth open.

It was as if he wanted to tell the Executioner something, but he dived face-first into the ground, never to rise again. Bolan saw a trio of men appear, wearing Khaki desert clothing and the distinctive blue berets and armbands of a UN security team.

"Identify yourself!" one of them said, aiming a Colt Commando at him.

"Colonel Stone, U.S. Army Criminal Investigation Division," he lied. He knew that he could rely on Captain Blake to provide him with some verification of his cover if push came to shove. Bolan didn't intend to cause any trouble with these men, not when he was here to help them out.

"Captain Rhodin," the one with the highest rank pips said. "Thank you for helping out."

Bolan scanned the man's face. He looked Arabic even with his eyes obscured by the shooting glasses. This was no big surprise considering that the UN usually did its best to hire people who could fit in and relate. But there was something wrong. "Anytime. I've been part of an investigation in the area involving the group behind this attack," Bolan said slowly.

Rhodin looked around for more marauders. His clean-shaven jaw was a shade lighter than the skin on his cheeks. The perception clicked into place, and Bolan recalled the name that the "UN security" man so casually tossed out—a name from Tera Geren's list.

Olsen Rhodin was the leader of the Abraham's Dagger cell that she was hunting. Bolan stiffened in recognition, his Uzi coming up.

More gunmen rushed in, their rifles erupting with automatic blasts of lead and fire. Bolan and the three imposters scattered. One man dived alongside the Executioner. The wall he'd stood in front of moments before was now pockmarked with a hundred new holes, but the charging enemy wasn't slowing down. They adjusted their aim, but not before the Executioner stiff-armed his machine pistol and swept them with withering blasts of his own cleansing fire. He knocked down three of the seven remaining attackers.

A form came darting from behind the hospital, his gun snorting and snarling like a chain saw. Marid Haytham opened fire on the last four marauders, catching them off balance. Totally focused on the downed Executioner, they were unprepared for a strike from the side. Bullets tore mercilessly through the men.

Bolan looked up and sought out the Abraham's Dagger intruders. "They're disguised as UN security forces," Bolan called to Haytham, pushing off the ground.

"Look out, Stone!" the Palestinian shouted back.

From the shout of alarm, Bolan knew what was coming. He ducked, avoiding having the back of his head crushed by the unyielding stock of an assault rifle. Tumbling forward on his shoulder, he looked to see one of the Israelis lunging at him, his face a grim mask of hatred.

Unfortunately, in his somersault, his already tenuous grasp on his Uzi was lost. The Abraham's Dagger commando stepped back, swinging the rifle around to aim at him.

The burst of autofire was blinding and deafening.

17

Marid Haytham brought his borrowed P-90 to bear on the man who was going to kill Colonel Brandon Stone. He triggered the weapon as he charged. The Israeli gunman saw the surge of movement and swung his muzzle. Out of the short barrel of his enemy's rifle, the muzzle-flash was a basketball-sized fireball, impressive to the Palestinian fighter even in broad daylight.

Haytham saw his bullets strike home. The shooter jerked almost in slow motion with each successive impact. But something was wrong. The Hamas man couldn't feel his legs anymore. Instead, a burning sensation boiled within his torso and his hands loosened on the P-90 submachine gun. The weapon sailed, spearing into the ground as momentum dragged him forward several stumbling steps.

Strong hands grabbed him and held him up. He looked into the face of Colonel Brandon Stone. He looked down and saw one side of his shirt drenched in blood.

"You've been hit," Bolan said, voice disjointed and muffled. "It's a lung shot. You can make it."

Haytham tried to swallow. Blood bubbled into his mouth. "You're bleeding too," he said.

"Old injuries," the American lied. "I need a medic!"

Haytham reached up, fingers clawing into Bolan's vest. "There's still two more. I saw them go inside."

"You're not going to die," the colonel ordered.

Haytham's eyes started to blur, but he blinked, bringing them back into focus. "Stop them. Save the innocent."

He heard the bubbling sound of a child's laughter. It could have been from the refugee camp, but it sounded so familiar. He turned to see where the sound came from, when he saw the stocky shape of a man, leveling a rifle at Stone's back. With his last vestiges of strength, the Palestinian swung him aside, literally throwing him six feet.

Haytham was impressed with the display of power, then looked down the barrel of the gun intended for the American. He didn't blink.

The black tunnel of the gun's muzzle became a glowing light.

THE EXECUTIONER'S Desert Eagle was in his fist three heartbeats after he recovered from being tossed like a sack of potatoes. Marid Haytham had saved his life twice in as many minutes. Now, he watched the Palestinian man convulse as bullets punched out from a window.

He fought off a nauseating wave of stunned shock and triggered the massive steel pistol, smashing glass. Feeble cracks of return fire poked at him, the dirt around him puffed as missed shots rained all around. Bolan scrambled to his feet, racing halfway to the window before he saw the gunman disappear into the halls of the hospital. He stopped and checked on Haytham. His eyes were open, staring glassily toward the blue sky.

He thumbed the dead man's eyes closed. There were a million things he wanted to say over the departed soul, but he remembered the final words whispered to him.

Stop them. Save the innocent.

The Executioner didn't have to be told twice. There was a

time to say words over the dead, but this wasn't one. He hit the door, reloading his Desert Eagle on the run.

Marid Haytham had finally been reunited with his family. He was at peace.

Mack Bolan, on the other hand, wondered when he would ever achieve that state.

TEARING HER ATTENTION from the injured Laith Khan, Tera Geren heard the sounds of renewed battle within the hospital. She looked through the clear-plastic magazine of her P-90 and was satisfied that she had thirty shots left to deal with a combat situation. Especially if Striker and Marid Haytham were still in the fight.

She looked back at Laith.

"Go! I'll be okay," Laith responded to her unspoken question.

Geren turned the corner and came face-to-face with the stocky, grim assassin she recognized instantly as Greb Steiner. She brought up her P-90, but the quarters were too close, and his big hand slapped up and under hers, pointing the weapon's muzzle into the ceiling as she triggered her first burst. Dust rained from shattered tiles, forcing them both to back off, partially blinded by the cloud that rushed down between them.

Trying to blink grit out of her eyes, she opened up with the P-90 again in blind rage. The stream of bullets was ineffective, and suddenly she folded over the biggest fist she ever felt, the air exploding from her lungs.

A wild swing brushed across her hair. Geren had taken her shots, now Greb Steiner was taking his own. Screams from behind warned her that she had to hold the line against the Abraham's Dagger marauder.

She reached out with a jab, striking heavy muscle, then felt something hard slam into her clavicle. Lights flashed in her head as once again the breath was knocked out of her.

The line she held was fraying with every heartbeat.

THE EXECUTIONER STALKED the hallway, Desert Eagle leading the way. While the prefab building was meant to provide as much space as possible for injured people to be wheeled into rooms, Bolan's long arms made it hard for him to turn a corner and keep his distance.

He didn't want to get into another wrestling match. His muscles ached, his bones creaked, and the blood seeping from the wound on his right arm made the blacksuit stick to his skin and crackle. His legs felt wobbly beneath him, and he knew that another life and death struggle would not be one in his favor, especially against someone fresh and ready for combat.

As he rounded a corner, he lurched to one side. Rhodin waited for him and opened fire the moment he caught sight of Bolan. He hit the floor, Desert Eagle spitting lead, but the Israeli moved like greased lightning.

Rhodin disappeared into an examination room. The doorjamb exploded under the jackhammer impacts of Bolan's .44 Magnum barrage. The Abraham's Dagger assassin leaned out and returned fire, the Colt Commando sending off shock waves of overpressure from its enormous muzzle-flash.

Bolan blinked away the glowing orange afterimage of the Colt Commando's fireball and saw that even Rhodin himself was staggered by the power of his own weapon. Bolan fired off two rounds. One smashed into the rifle's frame and ripped it from the Israeli's grasp. The second round clipped the man's side. Then the mighty pistol locked empty.

The Executioner wasn't going to make the mistake of charging. He held his ground, reaching for a spare magazine and reloading the big handcannon. He had the corner for cover, and he kept it. His arm ached, protesting spikes of pain driving up and down from his tortured muscle. He shifted the big Desert Eagle to his left hand and took a couple of deep breaths.

A blaze of autofire went off elsewhere in the building. The Executioner felt an urgent tug, his instincts demanding he take out Rhodin and help Geren with the other man, but Bolan's reason fought against it. It would have proved easy to pluck a grenade from his harness and lob it toward the examination room, but there was no guarantee that the exploding bomb would do anything more than harm a patient who might have been left behind.

Bolan's hand wrapped around the round shape of the smooth-skinned fragmentation grenade, thoughts suddenly whirling to the surface. A plan of action erupted in his brain.

The Executioner unhooked the little hellbomb and threw it, sailing it through the doorway where Rhodin had disappeared.

The pin still remained, leaving the weapon inert.

"Fuck!" Rhodin shouted and he dived out into the hallway, pistol up and flashing.

Bolan fired off two shots from his Desert Eagle, feeling the recoil shake up his arm, instants before he felt the thundering impact of a .44 Magnum slug against his own body armor. The wind seared from his lungs, burning in his throat. The Executioner's body armor was good, though. It stopped the slug from tearing through him. As it was, he still felt like he'd been smacked with a hammer.

Rhodin was on the floor, struggling to get to his feet, his own Desert Eagle in his fist. Bolan had forgotten that they had retrieved their pistols from the same storage cache. He swung his weapon to bear on the Israeli before he could reach his feet.

Instead of continuing to rise, the Abraham's Dagger assassin dropped to the floor, cutting loose with his .44 Magnum pistol. It was everything the Executioner could do to dive across the hall, coming to a halt behind the counter. He was sporting two new bruises under his Kevlar. The Israeli gunman was good on the trigger.

Bolan lunged, flipping himself over the counter, boots kicking out hard. Rhodin, who had stalked around the nursing station counter, was caught right in the middle. The two men crashed to the floor, the Executioner riding the man down.

Rhodin tried to bring up his gun hand, but Bolan smashed down hard with the barrel of the heavy .44 Magnum pistol, catching the Israeli across the face. Cheekbone collapsed under the impact of the three pound handgun. The lack of sharp corners at the muzzle didn't hamper the tearing of flesh as Bolan ground the front sight into Rhodin's right eye and tore the gun free from the pulpy mush that was the assassin's face.

The Abraham's Dagger commando howled in horror and clawed at the Executioner, trying to get him off his chest. Instead, Bolan twisted the Desert Eagle and hammered the butt of the big gun into Rhodin's forehead. Skin split under the heavy strike.

The Executioner followed up with a punch from his injured, weakened right arm, but it might as well have been a swat from a kitten's paw. The assassin squirmed and struggled under Bolan, his hand reaching for a knife in his vest.

Bolan pressed his right hand into Rhodin's knife wrist, pinning him down, but the commando wasn't giving up. The Executioner stuffed the barrel of the Desert Eagle up and under Rhodin's chin.

The assassin got his knife free, the point slicing across the Executioner's thigh, but it was only a scratch. It was the last thing the murderer did before Bolan triggered the Desert Eagle.

The warrior collapsed off Rhodin's chest, drained of almost every ounce of strength. He could have shut down and slept for weeks if given the chance, but there was still one more Israeli hit man out there. He grabbed a section of desk and pulled himself up, arms shuddering under his weight. He picked up the Desert Eagle, then fished through Rhodin's belt to get two more magazines for the handgun.

Twenty-four rounds in three magazines—enough for all but the most pitched of battles.

One foot ahead of the other, Bolan staggered out into the hall. His sense of direction led him toward the triage area where the physicians had dragged Laith Khan. He hoped he would find Geren there.

A gunshot went off, and he heard the sound of a woman grunting in pain.

Suddenly, Bolan's footsteps became running strides; the weight of the Desert Eagle in his fist seemed light as a feather. He charged around the corner and saw Greb Steiner with a small handgun, a Beretta to Bolan's tired eyes, still aimed at Tera Geren's bloodied forehead. The Israeli hit man saw Bolan arrive and brought up his pistol, firing a single shot that plunked into the Executioner's Kevlar body armor.

The big American barely felt the little .22-caliber round strike his chest, but he skidded to a halt out of survival reflex.

Steiner's stocky form bent low, one powerful arm scooped up the tiny form of Geren. She twisted, one arm rising reflexively to clutch at the Israeli assassin's muscular limb as it closed against her throat. Steel slid into Steiner's other beefy paw, a combat dagger similar to the one that had slit a shallow cut across Bolan's thigh.

The Executioner lowered his Desert Eagle, not trusting his wobbly limbs or his reflexes to get an accurate shot into

Steiner's skull before he managed to sever several arteries in Tera's neck.

Steiner, holding the stunned Tera, looked at Bolan.

"Disarm, and we'll settle this like men," the Israeli assassin growled.

Bolan looked at Tera. The bullet had pierced her forehead, and she looked in dire straights.

"Drop your pistol, and we'll face each other like true warriors," Steiner said. The light glinted off the shimmering steel at Tera's throat. Her glazed eyes rolled to meet Bolan's.

"Shoot...this fucker," she gritted. Her hands tried to clench into fists. One side of her mouth didn't move properly. She knew she was dying.

Bolan unclipped his belt, the Desert Eagle in its hip holster, and the thigh pouch for his rifle magazines fell away. His cold blue eyes never leaving the sad-looking gaze of the Abraham's Dagger killer. His eyes lit from within, joy reaching them finally. Bolan knew the type, always lamenting the lack of a proper enemy.

Steiner threw the knife aside and let Tera drop to the ground like a rag doll, a smirk crossing his face. "You'd fight for someone with Nazi blood running through her veins?"

"I'd fight for someone who's given her all for me," Bolan answered. "You made one little mistake, though."

Steiner shifted his stance, hands up in a guarding position. "What's that?"

"You're not worth the blood on my knuckles," the Executioner said, pulling out his tiny Beretta Tomcat. The gun fired instantly, .32 caliber slugs flying as fast as he could pull the small pistol's trigger. Steiner jerked under multiple impacts.

The Tomcat locked back empty, and Steiner dropped to his knees, coughing blood.

Steiner looked up as Bolan slowly walked forward, feeding a fresh magazine into the tiny Beretta, cold, deadly eyes staring down.

"You were supposed to—" Steiner began, but the Executioner punched two more shots that struck him dead center of his forehead. One lodged in bone, but the other shattered through, tearing into brain matter, killing him instantly.

The assassin slumped at Bolan's feet.

"Maybe that's your problem," he told the dead man, his voice weighing sadly, remembering the dead people this man's machinations had been responsible for. "You expected me to play by the rules."

Outside, he heard the thunder of helicopter rotors, and through the glass, he saw choppers soaring in, probably laden with Army Rangers or Marines. They would help secure Makaki against any further marauders.

He tossed the pistol and picked up the lifeless form of Tera Geren. He turned back to help the physicians with Laith Khan. For now, he'd had enough of killing.

It was time to nurture life.

PROMISE TO DEFEND

The elite counter-terrorist group known as Stony Man has one mandate: to protect good from evil; to separate those willing to live in peace from those who kill in order to fulfill their own agenda. When all hell breaks loose, the warriors of Stony Man enter the conflict knowing each battle could be their last, but the war against freedom's oppressors will continue....

STONY MAN.

*Available
October 2005
at your favorite retailer.*

SKYFIRE
Wind of a grim conspiracy comes to light, and the levels of treachery go deep into America's secret corridors of power. When the Cadre Project was created decades ago, it served to protect the U.S. government during the Cold War. Now it's a twisted, despotic vision commandeered by a man whose hunger for power is limitless, whose plan to manufacture terror and lay a false trail of blame across the globe may find America heading into all-out world war against the old superpowers.

James Axler
Outlanders®

CERBERUS STORM

SPOILS OF VICTORY

The baronial machine ruling post-apocalyptic America is no more, yet even as settlers leave the fortressed cities and attempt to build new lives in the untamed outlands, a deadly new struggle is born. The hybrid barons have evolved into their new forms, their avaricious scope expanding to encompass the entire world. Though the war has changed, the struggle for the Cerberus rebels remains the same: save humanity from its slavers.

DARK TERRITORY

Amidst the sacred Indian lands in Wyoming's Bighorn Mountains, a consortium with roots in preDark secrets is engaged in the excavation of ancient artifacts, turning the newly liberated outlands into a hellzone. Kane and the Cerberus warriors organize a strike against the outlaws, only to find themselves navigating a twisted maze of legend, manipulation and the fury of a woman warrior. Driven by power, hatred and revenge, she's now on the verge of uncovering and releasing a force of unfathomable evil....

Available November 2005 at your favorite retailer.

TAKE 'EM FREE

2 action-packed novels plus a mystery bonus

NO RISK
NO OBLIGATION TO BUY

DEATH LANDS®

James Axler

DEATH LANDS

Ritual Chill

Ritual Chill

Cursed in fathomless ways, the future awaits...

STRANGE QUARRY

A cold sense of déjà vu becomes reality as Ryan's group emerges from a gateway they'd survived before—a grim graveyard of lost friends and nightmares. The consuming need to escape the dangerous melancholy of the place forces the company out into the frozen tundra, where an even greater menace awaits. The forbidding land harbors a dying tribe, cursed members of the ancient Inuit, who seize the arrival of Ryan and his band as their last hope to appease angry gods...by offering them up as human sacrifice.

In the Deathlands, the price for survival is the constant fear of death.

Available September 2005 at your favorite retail outlet.

GOLD EAGLE®

GDL71